CW01645999

WICKED STORM

A SAM WICK UNIVERSE THRILLER #1

CHASE AUSTIN

THRILLVERSE PUBLISHING

ABOUT WICKED STORM

A kidnapped girl. A human auction. One man against the traffickers.

Sam Wick is the one the Government calls on to extract people out of the worst of the worst enemy places on earth. Where the government cannot and will not go, he will. There is no guarantee that he'll succeed every time but he doesn't have a choice or does he?

What Readers are saying about Sam Wick's Adventures;

> ★★★★★ *"One heck of an entertaining and intense ride... Fast, entertaining, suspenseful and action-packed... you will find yourself flying through and it will be hard to let it go!" - Amazon Review*
>
> ★★★★★ *"...Fast paced read with a Kick-Ass hero you can't help rooting for." - Amazon Review*

★★★★★ *"...Full of awesome action. I can't wait to read the next book. I highly recommend you read this book..." - Amazon Review*

★★★★★ *"Wild action in a compact book." - Amazon Review*

★★★★★ *"Fast paced, lots of thrills. Highly entertaining." - Amazon Review*

★★★★★ *"Can't wait to read more by Chase." - Goodreads Review*

★★★★★ *"Interesting character and story line." - Amazon Review*

★★★★★ *"This book is a quick, thrilling, and enjoyable read." - Amazon Review*

GET YOUR FREEBIES

Do not Forget to download your FREE Books at

www.thechaseaustin.com

PROLOGUE

RIGHT NOW, **Someplace in Tirana, Albania**

"And now we present to you the most spectacular offering from our treasures of beauty," the emcee announced, his right hand clutching the mic and his left slicing through the air like he was conducting an orchestra. His voice squeaked into the mic and came out booming. This was his show, and the audience clung to his every word. With the camera crew focused on him, he was ready to deliver his life's best performance.

The murmuring in the hall had stopped. All eyes were on the stage. The entire arena was wrapped in darkness. Only the podium at the front left corner of the stage stood in an oasis of light.

Marco raised the wineglass and tilted it gently to his lips. The opaque purple liquid was a 1992 Screaming Eagle Cabernet Sauvignon from the Napa Valley; at five hundred grand, it was one of the world's finest and costliest wines. His eyes closed in ecstasy as the wine warmed his taste buds. He flicked a finger, and the man standing behind him switched on a 50-inch TV screen showing a live feed of the auction taking place on the floor below. He rarely attended these auctions in person, even though this was his property and this was his game.

The auctions he conducted here were like no other. The product could only be sold when there were two or more interested parties because of what came after.

When someone placed a winning bid, he would then have to fight for the product on sale, either in person or through an appointed proxy, in a cage match, a fight to the death between the contenders, which was equally, if not more, popular than the bidding process itself. The one who emerged victorious had the ultimate authority on the product being sold. This unique proposition had made Marco and his little game what it was today. It not only gave him the option to price his products higher than the market rate but also made the entire event a massive success among wealthy clients. So much so that there was a long waiting list to be in that room. The logistics were all handled by an efficient team working behind the scenes round the clock. Everything operated on autopilot, and Marco rarely needed to be in the hall for the game.

But today was different. Today he was here to watch the last auction of the night. *The auction of a US Senator's seventeen-year-old daughter.*

CHAPTER 1

22 HOURS AGO, **Athens International Airport Eleftherios Venizelos, Greece.**

The plane met the tarmac, wobbled slightly, and then steadied. The passengers didn't notice. It was four in the morning, and they were catching every last ounce of sleep they could before they hit the long queues at the immigration counter.

The flight attendant, dressed impeccably with multiple layers of makeup with not one hair out of place, stood with the in-flight phone in her hand. But before beginning her last announcement of the night, she managed a forced smile at the passengers in the front-middle rows, some of whom were awake and looking at her expectantly. A bunch of kids. Clearly not frequent fliers. She glazed her eyes over every other passenger and focused on the back of the head of her fellow air hostess standing at the end of the aisle.

. . .

"Ladies and gentlemen, welcome to Eleftherios Venizelos International Airport. Local time is 4 AM, and the temperature outside is sixty-two degrees. For your safety and comfort, please remain seated with your seat belt fastened until the Captain turns off the fasten seat belt sign. You may now use your cell phones if you wish. Please check around your seat for any personal belongings you may have brought on board with you, and please use caution when opening the overhead bins, as heavy articles may have shifted around during the flight.

If you require deplaning assistance, please remain in your seat until all other passengers have deplaned. One of our crew members will then be pleased to assist you. On behalf of Etihad Airways and the entire crew, I'd like to thank you for joining us on this trip, and we look forward to seeing you onboard again soon. Have a nice day!"

The kids in the front middle rows—three boys and three girls, all in their late teens—had been planning this trip for ages. Their first independent overseas trip with no elders to interfere with their plans.

Mia's eighteenth birthday had presented them the perfect opportunity to finally put their plans into action.

For Mia, this trip was less a matter of going on a vacation with friends than of getting out from under the protective shadow of her father, Brian Reed.

. . .

A well-known US senator, Reed had always been very protective of his daughter ever since her mother succumbed to colon cancer.

In fact, he had chosen Mia's college just for the fact that its dean was Reed's childhood friend. Through him, Reed could keep tabs on Mia. That was the reason she had made sure that the dean, too, didn't have a clue about this trip.

She wasn't a spoilt child, but her father sometimes did get on her nerves. She knew he had her best interests in mind, but at times she felt that she was the sensible one among the two when it came to things like personal space and freedom.

But freedom wasn't the only thing she was looking forward to on this trip.

She was on this trip with five of her friends, and one of them was Troy. And he was the reason she didn't want this trip to end ever.

From that first sight of him, Mia's life had taken a one-hundred-and-eighty-degree turn in just a few months.

Her father had always admonished her not to focus on anything other than academics, but as soon as she'd got into college, something had changed. Something massive.

Everything that had seemed so important once, like choosing which electives to take during her freshman year, suddenly became trivial.

She wasn't naïve, but even then, she couldn't possibly have imagined what lay ahead of her. And it had all happened with that one look.

She hadn't known Troy's name at the time, but from that first encounter, he had changed her life in ways nothing in her life so far had prepared her for.

The movies she'd watched as a teen seemed to turn real, and those ridiculous plotlines suddenly started making sense.

She still didn't know how or why it had happened. It wasn't as if Troy was the first guy she had ever seen or met, but some things defy explanation. Apart from her father, no other man had made such an impression on her. She at times felt so utterly lost in the moment of passion that her judgment was clouded, and all she could see was Troy. But he didn't know that, and she hadn't explored her feelings in much depth either. They were both still undecided if they were just friends or something more.

. . .

This trip was just another step in their blossoming relationship, or maybe more.

CHAPTER 2

THE PLANE CAME to a stop at the gate, and the deboarding process began. Up and down the aisle, passengers were getting up to retrieve their luggage from the overhead bins.

Troy, who was sitting beside a sleeping Mia, had taken out his cell phone as soon as the announcement was made. While waiting to regain connectivity, he turned to check on the others sitting in the row behind them.

Dan and Lisa were still asleep. Lucas and Charlotte were not. He smiled as Lucas pumped his fist in the air, excited to finally land after one hell of a long flight.

Troy turned back to Mia.

. . .

Her head was leaning against the window, and her hair covered her face partially, creating a veil that made her look ethereal. Troy lifted the strands gently from her face. She murmured softly but remained fast asleep. He felt a sudden urge to kiss her but stopped himself.

Troy was still watching her face when he felt a hand on his shoulder. It was Lucas nudging him to get going. Troy looked around. The plane was almost empty. Dan and Lisa were up too, checking their seats for things they might have dropped beneath their seats.

Troy turned back to Mia and rubbed her shoulder gently. "Get up," he said softly.

Mia stirred reluctantly, and Troy nudged her again before she could go back to sleep. This time she relented and opened her eyes. Her gaze landed on Lucas first and then on Troy.

"We landed?" she asked.

"Eons ago." Lucas grinned. "The captain is waiting for you to get up so he can have his breakfast or dinner or whatever."

Mia made a face as she adjusted her clothes and straightened her back. Troy got up to retrieve their bags from the overhead bins.

. . .

"Why there is no word for a meal between dinner and breakfast, it could be 'Dinfast.' I can totally see it catching on." Lucas was still in his own world.

"Shut... up... Lucas," Mia said, getting up.

"Make me."

Annoying Mia was Lucas's favorite pastime. Troy grinned, seeing them taunting each other.

The overhead bin was already open. Only Mia's and his bags were left to be taken down. His was a simple backpack, but Mia's bag was loaded. He dragged it to the seat beside them. Lucas watched him but made no move to help.

"Lucas!" Mia admonished.

"What?"

"Help him."

. . .

"This is all part of the boyfriend-girlfriend package. He and only he has the right to drag your suitcase. So, bite me," Lucas teased.

Mia blushed, and so did Troy, but he hid it in the guise of handling bags. Mia couldn't. *You're an ass,* she mouthed at Lucas and got up.

It seemed like everyone was sure of their relationship except themselves.

Charlotte, Dan, and Lisa were already near the gate, waiting for the three of them.

"Are you guys coming or not?" Charlotte's voice echoed in the empty plane.

It had an instant effect on Lucas, and he straightened as if someone had tightened his leash.

"Comin' babes," he responded, grabbing his bags.

"The boss summons," Mia said with a laugh. Lucas gave her a mock glare but hurried down the aisle.

. . .

"Right behind you, bulldog." Mia chirped. Lucas fumed but said nothing.

"We are the only ones left," Troy said to Mia in a flirtatious tone.

It was their thing. They flirted with each other, but neither had moved beyond that. Perhaps now, they would. Her dream vacation had just started.

"They are staring at us. Move now." Mia nudged him. She was right. The usually friendly flight attendants were shooting looks of exasperation their way.

Troy sighed and dragged the bags towards the exit. Mia followed him.

"Thanks." The flight attendant gave them a strained smile as they crossed the threshold. Troy ignored her. Mia smiled back at her before exiting.

CHAPTER 3

6:30 AM

To say that that the immigration queue was sluggish would have been a massive understatement, and when the six of them finally reached the counter, it was already over two hours since their flight had landed.

The immigration officer on the other side of the desk looked at them with disdain. They could practically hear him thinking, 'Another group of teenage morons. Lucas wanted to respond to this imaginary insult, but Charlotte preempted his move with just a *look*. Dan and Lisa were too sleepy to care about what the immigration officer thought about them or their American descent. Mia and Troy were only waiting for the torture to get over.

"Passports?" the IO demanded.

. . .

Charlotte, who had already collected all six passports, slid them through the small glass window. The IO slowly checked each of them on a desktop that looked like it was from the nineties and ran on the slowest processor ever built. It took ages for every passport to be checked and stamped. With every passport, the IO asked the person to step forward as he matched the face with the passport photo.

When Mia's name was called, the IO took extra time to check if everything was in order. No one noticed that once the IO was sure, he glanced at the man standing on his side of the counter but at a distance and gave a slight nod. The man, bald and tattooed, watched Mia from behind the glass and nodded back.

"Business or pleasure?" the IO asked.

"Pleasure... just pleasure." It was Lucas who answered. He was next in line and getting impatient.

"We are here on vacation, officer. Sorry about my friend," Mia said, embarrassed when she saw the IO's facial muscles tense. Troy put a hand on Lucas's shoulder, gesturing to him to control his verbal diarrhoea. Lucas may be a rock star at college, but not here.

"Where will you be staying?"

. . .

"Athens-Marina hotel," Mia responded. The hotel was her choice from all the options they had weighed in.

"Thank you, and welcome to Athens." The officer took a couple of minutes more before finally handing over the passport to Mia.

In all, the immigration formalities took about twenty minutes for all six of them, but it felt like an eternity. Finally, they were through immigration and free to roam in Greece for the next seventy-two hours.

When they got out of the airport, it was seven in the morning.

"I now pronounce this vacation officially begun. Booyah!" Lucas threw up his arms and yelled so loudly that people around them turned to look.

Mia and Troy glanced sideways in embarrassment, Charlotte was red with rage, and Dan and Lisa were still too sleepy to give a damn.

"Lucas!" Charlotte gritted her teeth.

"Yes, baby." Lucas smiled. He lowered his arms and wrapped them around her waist.

. . .

"Don't baby me." She tried to get away from him, but his grip was solid. She resisted, then gave in, but not without warning. "If you do this one more time, I don't know you."

"Okay, baby." Lucas gave her a peck on the shoulder, followed by a toothy smile. They both knew his smile always worked like a charm.

"Don't."

"Don't what?" Lucas gave her another peck on the cheek.

"Mia." Charlotte looked at Mia and Lisa for help.

"Leave me out of this. I don't know you both." Mia said, and everyone except Charlotte chuckled, even Dan and Lisa.

A voice broke into their laughter. "Sir, hotel?" A cab had halted near them, and the cabbie was leaning out of the window expectantly.

CHAPTER 4

"ID CONFIRMED. IT'S HER." The bald, tattooed man was now near the airport exit gate. His eyes centered on Mia, standing some fifty yards away, waiting for a cab along with her friends. She had her back to him, but he could still see her side profile. She was wearing a crop top and a pair of blue jeans. Her persona symbolized the carefree spirit of adulthood. The rest of her band was ditto - a carefree group of teens, ecstatic about their first foreign trip.

The man knew everything about all six of them. He had spent his last forty-eight hours doing nothing except digging up everything about the lives of these six teens. Their names, ages, home addresses, likes, dislikes, parents, parent's occupation, and everything he could lay his hands on about their private lives. Social media was the gateway to it. There was nothing these dumb-ass kids didn't promptly share online, except maybe their nudes.

. . .

And now, when his target was right before him, he had to find a way to separate her from the rest of the gang. Well, that was the preferred mode, but if not, then there was another option too. It would be messy, but he would still consider it a success.

"I need proof," the man at the other end responded.

"On its way." The bald man checked his phone and sent the photos he had taken since Mia's identity was confirmed at the immigration desk.

He didn't know the name of the person he was speaking to, but the only thing that mattered was that he worked for Marco. That solely was more than enough. It also meant that the bald man couldn't fail in his assignment. There was no place in the world where he and his family could hide from Marco.

There was a lull in their conversation as the photos were received and examined.

"Good." Marco's man finally spoke.

"They're staying at the Athens-Marina Hotel," the bald man added.

"You have men there?"

. . .

"Yes."

"You know where to deliver the package?"

"Yes."

"You have ten hours. Get it done in less."

"I know."

"Mirë mbetesh."

"Mirë mbetesh," the bald man replied in Albanian and disconnected.

CHAPTER 5

THE SIX TEENS stared at the cab. It wasn't in the best of shape or any shape at all. It was, in fact, not even a taxi but a crumbling minivan.

"This thing can run?" Lucas shot a wisecrack.

The driver took this as a yes. "Hundred miles speed, sir. Ferrari of Athens," he said, with a gullible smile.

His tone and smile made everyone chuckle.

"Sir, you are laughing now, but once you get in, you see that I'm right."

"You mean six people with tons of luggage?" Troy said.

. . .

"No worries, sir. People inside, luggage on top."

"Top?" This time it was Lucas.

"Rooftop, sir, rooftop." The driver gestured at the luggage carrier on the van's roof.

They looked around. There was no other cab. They were eager to get to the hotel, and this seemed to be their only available option.

"You know this hotel?" Troy showed the cabbie the hotel address on his cell phone.

"Athens-Marina Hotel! Yes, sir. Friendly hotel. I'll take you." The driver smiled and opened the passenger side door. He then walked around and opened the back door.

The minivan had three rows of seats. Before anyone could think what to do, Dan yelled, "Shotgun." It was as if someone had thrown a bucket of ice-cold water on him, yanking him from his sleep. The girls looked at each other and quickly decided that the middle seat was for them. That left Troy and Lucas with smelly back seats with zero air circulation.

CHAPTER 6

IT TOOK a few minutes for the driver to load the luggage on the overhead luggage carrier. Lucas and Troy stood outside as the others made themselves comfortable in the van.

Watching the driver huffing and puffing as he lifted their heavy suitcases and backpacks was a painful sight. Finally, Troy stepped forward to lend him a helping hand. He didn't want a driver with a broken back. Lucas let out an audible groan before moving forward to help too.

"Thank you, sir." The driver gave them a toothy smile as he adjusted the last bag.

"Is it done?" Lisa asked what everyone else inside the van wanted to know too. They had had enough of watching the driver's hairy belly peeking from under his t-shirt every time he stretched to put another bag on the carrier.

. . .

"Yes, yes." It was the driver again, oblivious to the disgusted faces his passengers were making seeing his belly.

Troy and Lucas looked at each other before taking the plunge of sitting in the back seat. They hoped it would be a short journey.

Troy checked his phone. It was seven-twenty am.

"How far is the hotel?" Lucas asked.

"Not far." The driver replied without understanding the meaning of the question.

"He means when will we reach?" Dan explained.

"For that, we have to start first." The driver chuckled at his statement.

"So, start." Dan sounded annoyed.

"Yes, sir," the driver said, flustered at Dan's tone.

. . .

The van's engine coughed once, and the tires rolled forward without hesitation. The driver knew the vehicle well. The sense of movement and the airflow gave everyone a sense of relief.

Exiting the airport was the first milestone.

The sun was still not ruthless, and, being a Saturday morning, the roads were yet not clogged with traffic.

Forty minutes into the drive, the driver's cell phone rang.

“YA til'ky vykhodzhu z aeroportu.” He spoke in a language that wasn't English, and Dan's senses heightened. He had researched extensively before embarking on this trip, more than anyone else in the group. He had seen all kinds of documentaries and movies about Greece and read in horror about gullible foreigners being taken for a ride abroad. The problem was whenever he tried to discuss this with the rest of the gang, all he got were rolling eyes and the one line he had tired of hearing by now: "Calm down, Dan!" But he was proud that he was at least familiar with rudimentary Greek, which he was sure would save them a load of trouble on this trip. But right now, whatever the driver was speaking, it definitely wasn't Greek.

A shrill voice came from the other side. Probably a woman.

. . .

"Akumulyator telefonu zapovnenyy," the driver responded in an annoyed tone. "Так, Так." He turned to Dan suddenly and said, "What time, sir?"

"Huh."

"Time," the driver repeated, indicating Dan's watch.

"Eight," Dan replied hesitantly, then looked over his shoulder at the five sitting behind. The girls were busy chatting amongst themselves. Troy and Lucas looked pale as if they were not getting any air.

Lucas especially was trying to suck as much air as possible from a small hole in the back window. None of them were paying any attention to the driver's conversation.

The driver listened to whatever he was being told, then smiled before responding, "YA doberusʹ do hotelyu Athens-Marina Hotel o 8:30. Zvidty ya pryydu dodomu." And disconnected the call.

For some time, no one spoke, and then Dan's curiosity overcame his hesitation.

"How much more time?"

. . .

"Fifteen minutes, sir."

"To the hotel?" Dan confirmed.

"Yes, sir." The driver smiled.

"Was that your wife?"

"Who, sir?"

"On the phone."

"Yes, sir. She was asking about my breakfast. I told her I'd come home after dropping you off at the hotel."

"Oh... you are not Greek?" Dan asked.

"Greek? No, sir."

Dan waited for him to say which country he came from, but when nothing came, he had to prod, "Then?"

"Ukraine."

. . .

"Ukraine?"

"My country."

"Uhuh."

Dan relaxed and the rest of the trip passed in silence.

"We reached, sir." The driver said, reducing the speed.

That was music to their ears. It had been a long trip, and now all they wanted was the comfort of some good food and a comfy bed to catch some rest before they partied nonstop over the next couple of days.

The van turned right to a secluded street. Contrary to the hustle-bustle of the city, the road seemed as if it was in a different town. The calm and quiet were enticing. The right side of the street had a twelve feet high wall with barbed wire on the top, and the left side was capped with a row of large, old trees.

The cab entered the hotel and settled in its parking lot. The six passengers looked out and saw a decent-sized board to their right that read 'Athens-Marina' in Greek and English.

. . .

Dan got out of the cab the moment it came to a halt. The three girls got out happily from the second row, followed by Troy and Lucas, who were just happy to get shots of fresh air.

The guard at the entrance rang for the bellboy while also greeting the six of them.

The bellboy, after a quick greeting, went on to help the driver to unload the luggage from the roof rack.

The others counted their bags as Mia paid the driver. "Keep the change." she said.

"Thank you, ma'am," the driver replied. Within seconds after that, he was out of the hotel premises, probably on his way to breakfast.

CHAPTER 7

ENTERING THE RECEPTION AREA, the six friends were surprised to see the simple decor of the hotel. There was a couch to their left, the reception desk to their right, and the elevator in front of them. Behind the reception desk was a single staffer, watching the six guests. As their eyes fell on him, he smiled as if he was posing for a photo, though his eyes remained still. It was a habitual routine, and he probably found no joy in doing it any longer.

Troy stepped forward. "We have a booking."

"Sure, sir. In the name of?"

"Amelia Reed." Mia joined Troy at the reception desk with her ID held upfront.

. . .

"Sure, ma'am." The man looked up the reservation on his computer, matched it with Mia's ID, and nodded. "Three rooms. Ma'am, please ask your friends to share their IDs to complete the process."

Mia gestured to the others who came forward with their IDs. The man diligently entered the details in his system, then picked up the phone and spoke into it.

After some yesses, nos, and some nodding, he put the receiver down and looked at them apologetically.

"Ma'am, the rooms are not yet ready. It's too early for check-in. May I suggest that you all should wait in the hotel's restaurant? We will serve breakfast soon."

"How long will the rooms take?"

"A couple of hours." The man sounded apologetic.

Mia looked at Troy and the others. Everyone was suddenly looking more exhausted. The hotel decor and the wait had dampened the mood.

"Can you get it done faster?" Troy asked.

. . .

"I'll try, sir, but it will still take an hour or so. I'll send someone to you when the rooms are ready. I will move your luggage to the rooms. You can go and relax at the restaurant. The breakfast is complimentary."

"Complimentary means free?" Lucas asked with a twinkle in his eyes.

"Yes, sir." The manager said with earnestness.

"Great." Lucas jumped at the offer. "Where's the restaurant?"

"First floor. You can use the elevator." He pointed to the elevator at the end of the lobby.

"Thanks," By the time Mia could finish her sentence, Lucas was already flying towards the elevator.

When the elevator opened on the first floor, they almost choked in surprise—this was better than the reception area.

Way better!

Maybe whatever was below was just the security screening.

. . .

The Mediterranean inspired the spacious lobby; from the terra-cotta tiles to the high ceiling fans, they could well be in the Balearic Isles. The space was bright and airy. The music in the background was soft, and the colors gentle to the eye. The restaurant was at the end of the lobby, to the right.

When they entered the restaurant, it was empty. Though not yet open, the buffet had already been laid out and looked mouth-watering to the tired, hungry souls.

"Thanks, Mia, for choosing this place rather than going with what we had suggested," Lucas said, gazing at all the food.

The rest of the gang had the same thoughts.

CHAPTER 8

8:15 AM

A uniformed staffer approached them. He had got a call from the reception manager already. "Welcome to Athens-Marina. Please have a seat. Breakfast will be served in about fifteen minutes. The restrooms are on that side if you want to freshen up." The man had short-cropped hair, a neat beard, and the sleeve of his white shirt partially covered a tattoo on the right wrist. The smile plastered on his face looked forced.

"Fifteen minutes, you said?" Lucas asked.

"Yes, sir."

"Great." Lucas moved towards the restrooms. Everyone else followed suit.

As the group disappeared into the restrooms, the uniformed staffer took out his cell phone and typed a short message: "Target is in the restaurant."

In a Toyota SUV parked some five hundred yards from the hotel at a spot that wasn't covered by the hotel's CCTV cameras, Ylli - a man in a navy-blue t-shirt and reflector shades reached with his tattoo-covered right arm for the phone vibrating on the dashboard.

"Sekret has sent the message," Ylli said to Erag, his companion in Greek. "About time. This wait is killing me. I didn't sleep all night because of this assignment." Ylli was the one following the group from the airport. He had now changed his airport staff uniform and sported a more casual look.

Erag grunted irritably. "Stop cribbing. Get coffee or something." He scanned the street once more out of habit. Besides the hotel, there were no other commercial establishments on the road. Instead, trees and plain tracts of farms surrounded them. They knew that the scantily populated region and the hotel's lax security would work to their advantage.

The Toyota had followed the cab from the airport, keeping a safe distance, and Erag was sure of no one noticing them.

. . .

"You need to get us better assignments," Ylli continued in the same complaining tone. "The payout isn't enough."

Erag turned to him. "Why don't you tell that to Marco, huh? You know he spared our lives last time only because we agreed to repay him in the manner and time of his choosing. Deliver this package to his men, and we'll be done. Let's get the hell out of this city then."

Ylli said nothing. He knew Erag was right. He had thought of the same, but every time, some or the other thing stopped him.

"The auction is tonight," Erag reminded him.

"I know." Ylli's tone was less complaining now.

"Then know also that this will be over soon."

Ylli was still irritated but said nothing. He knew Marco was trouble and not someone he wanted to piss off.

CHAPTER 9

9:05 AM, **Athens Marina Hotel**

When the breakfast buffet finally opened, Lucas was ready with his plate. The other followed him. Being the only guests this early in the morning had its perks. The service was responsive and courteous.

The food tasted heavenly, especially to tastebuds accustomed to college mess food.

"Your rooms are ready," Sekret informed the group as they were on the last legs of their breakfast.

Troy nodded in acknowledgment as everyone else was busy digging into the dessert.

. . .

Ten minutes later, the group was finally done and ready to retire to their rooms when Sekret approached them again. "This is for you." He handed them three gift-wrapped boxes—one for each room.

"What's this?"

"A welcome gift from the hotel for your stay here," Sekret replied with a plastered smile.

"It's not necessary...." Mia said

"...but thank you." Lucas swooped forward and grabbed a box.

"You're welcome," Sekret said and handed the rest of the two to Troy, who had to take it.

"Our luggage has been taken to the rooms?" Lisa reconfirmed.

"Yes, it's been kept in one of your rooms, and before I forget, these are your access cards." He handed them three cards. "Third floor. Please use the elevator."

"Thanks." Dan smiled and turned towards the elevator.

. . .

Sekret stood by politely as they entered the elevator. As soon as the elevator doors closed behind them, he took out his cell phone and sent another message.

CHAPTER 10

9:37 AM, **Athens Marina Hotel**

The elevator opened into a well-lit lobby on the third floor.

A hotel staffer was waiting patiently for them in the lobby. Their luggage was piled beside him, still in the lobby and not in the room like the restaurant staffer had told them.

The bellboy led them to their rooms, two of which were adjacent to each other, and the third faced them.

"This is your luggage," the bellboy said.

They glanced at it and quickly made a note of their bags. Everything was in order.

. . .

Dan thanked the man.

"Enjoy your stay," the man said and left.

"This is us." Charlotte marched over and put her hand on the door of the room that was across, as soon as the man entered the elevator.

"No, that will be our room," Lisa countered.

Lucas, Dan, and Troy looked at each other. This could get out of hand. They had to do something. "Let Mia decide," Dan said.

"What?" the three girls spoke almost in unison. "Why?"

"This hotel was her choice, and it's also her birthday," Dan said.

"That's still a few hours away," Charlotte said a little peevishly.

"There is a tie, and she is a neutral party." Dan smiled innocently.

"How?" Lisa asked but at the same time as Charlotte.

. . .

"Fine." Charlotte had agreed just because not only Mia was her roommate but also her best friend.

With Charlotte giving in, Lisa too nodded her agreement.

"So, whatever Mia decides will be final," Dan said.

They all turned to her. Mia stared back blankly. She knew that she would not look good any which way. She glanced at Troy for support, but he shrugged helplessly.

Mia sighed. "Lisa, why do you want this room?" she asked.

"Privacy," Lisa said. "These two rooms share a wall, and I don't want to hear Lucas's grunts even if it's only for four seconds."

"Four seconds! Are you crazy, girl?" Lucas was offended. "Tell her, Charlotte."

"Yes, Lisa. How dare you? It's four and a half." Charlotte smiled.

"What! Now you see, lady. Now you see." Lucas was now doubly offended.

. . .

"Charlotte, why do you want this room?" Mia asked Charlotte, ignoring Lucas's ramblings.

"Same as Lisa, but in Dan's case, I think it will be...."

"Yeah, yeah, I get it. You are going to say some random shitty number like five seconds," Dan said, raising his hands.

Charlotte grinned. "I was going to say ten minutes, but you know best. Five seconds it is." Everyone burst out laughing.

"So, if it's a matter of just four or five seconds, then I guess you both deserve each other. Troy and I will be in this room," Mia declared.

Troy grinned. Everyone else had a what-just-happened look on their faces, and Dan was the center of their ire. It was, after all, his reasoning that Mia would be a neutral judge.

"I call dibs on this room," Lucas blurted, going to one of the adjacent rooms, studiously avoiding Charlotte's glare. He knew she would be blaming him for not supporting her enough.

"Whatever," Dan said and walked over to the other room.

. . .

"We won," Lucas mouthed the words to Charlotte.

"Fuck off." Charlotte pushed the door open and dragged her luggage inside.

"You said four-and-a-half," Lucas complained, following her.

"See you in the evening," Troy called as he and Mia entered their room.

In each of the three-room, the welcome gifts they had been handed in the restaurant were tossed carelessly on the side table and forgotten.

Inside each box was a small plush toy with a hidden listening device ready to transmit every sound coming from the three rooms.

CHAPTER 11

10:29 AM

Mia and Troy's room wasn't huge, but the large windows made it seem airy and expansive. The king-size bed at the center of the room's main wall took up most of the space. The white sheets looked inviting. Next, Mia peeked into the bathroom. With a jacuzzi bathtub and hot water, it didn't disappoint.

Inside the room, there was also a coffee table and chairs, but Troy and Mia knew that they would eat everything in bed. That had been their plan even before they boarded their flight.

This was the first time they were staying together. Everything was new, scary, and exciting at the same time.

Troy was the first one to get in the bathroom. Mia let him because she planned to take her own sweet time when her turn came. She started unpacking her things. By the time Troy came out, she had already placed her bag in the room's cupboard.

Troy was only in a towel. His athletic body glistening with water. She felt awkward looking at him.

"You did the unpacking," he said, sensing her discomfort.

"Uh... yeah." She said clumsily.

"What's in the box?" Troy sensed her nervousness and tried to change the topic.

"I don't know." Mia had forgotten all about the gift box.

"I'll check it. You want to freshen up?" Troy asked.

"Yeah... yeah." Mia winced inside. He must think her dumb. It was as if words had deserted her.

Grabbing the clothes she'd laid out on the bed, she walked towards the restroom with lowered eyes. Troy was standing in the way, and she turned sideways to slip past him. He didn't move, and her body rubbed against his wet body. His head turned as Mia moved past him. She raised her eyes to look into his and then immediately blushed.

Inside, she looked at herself in the mirror and found her cheeks red and a smile on her lips. She was in love, and the feeling was beyond words.

The moment she stepped under the showerhead, she realized how tired her body was. She stood under the hot water and felt some of her tiredness dissipate from her muscles.

Slowly, her mind drifted to her most pressing problem.

What was going to happen once she got out of the bathroom? The time when she would be alone in the room with Troy.

She tried to calm her nerves, but every thought that came to mind seemed to have the exact opposite effect on her. Suddenly, she realized with a start that she'd stayed in the shower for much longer than she'd intended to. She still had to run a razor over her legs.

CHAPTER 12

SIX MONTHS **ago**

Mia still remembered the first time she saw him. She had entered her dorm room to find the dark-haired boy leaning against the wall. Hair pushed back off his forehead, arms covered in tattoos, green eyes keenly watching everything yet seeming aloof. He was tall and lean, and Mia just couldn't stop herself from staring at him until her roommate Charlotte nudged her hard and made the introductions.

Troy was Lucas's friend and had tagged along when Lucas came over to meet Charlotte. However, that first meeting had been unusual as Troy had remained quiet and aloof, rolling his eyes in annoyance at Lucas's jokes and mostly checking his cell phone.

Today

As she wrapped a towel around her wet body, she heard a song, probably from the TV in the room. The lyrics were inaudible, but the music made her smile, imagining Troy getting bored in the room without her.

She still had to blow-dry her hair. She had planned for this moment for months, but all she saw now was a nervous wreck looking at her in the bathroom mirror.

CHAPTER 13

"WHAT'S THAT SOUND?" Erag asked.

"Probably the TV," Ylli responded.

Erag and Ylli were still in the SUV, listening intently to a small speaker catching signals from the listening devices in Troy and Mia's room. It had taken them some time, but they had finally latched on to the right device out of the three.

They had initially planned to plant the toy with the listening devices in the room even before the group arrived, but the assignment was so last-minute that the logistics of doing that had been virtually impossible. In addition, the two men had no link inside the hotel except Sekret, and he worked in the restaurant with no access to the guest rooms. So, they had come up with the idea of the gifts and then tried to latch on to the right one by trial and error. A roundabout way, but it had worked, and that was all that mattered.

The room had been awfully quiet so far, and that had made them nervous but hearing the song somewhat soothed their nerves.

CHAPTER 14

MIA CAME out of the bathroom in a short nightdress she had bought just for the trip. She found Troy standing in front of the TV with the remote in his hand, channel-surfing.

He was wearing only a pair of tight yellow shorts. She glanced at his incredible body, then quickly looked away. Troy saw her and turned off the TV.

"It was a toy."

"What?"

"The gift box... had a toy," Troy said, indicating the open box on the coffee table.

. . .

Mia nodded absent-mindedly as she gazed at his naked upper body covered with tattoos.

"Did they hurt?" She asked the one stupid question she'd always wanted to ask him.

"These?" Troy smiled when he saw her checking out his tattoos. "Only the first one, and not as bad as you would think. It's almost like a bee sting. No. Wait. Many bee-stings."

"Sounds terrible!" she exclaimed, and Troy laughed. Mia's eyes were still fixed on the tattoos.

"You can touch them if you want," Troy offered, and Mia flushed. They were both oddly unfamiliar with each other despite knowing each other for a few months, which seemed strangely comforting.

"You want to catch some sleep?" Troy asked.

Mia glanced at the king-size bed in the room, and multiple scenarios crossed her mind in an instant. She had thought about it millions of times in the past months, but now the reality of it struck her hard.

"We can use a pillow wall," Troy said as if he had read her mind.

. . .

"No... it's okay." Mia didn't want to sound uptight. It was she who had chosen the room, knowing that she would share it with Troy.

"Then we can cuddle. I'm a pretty good cuddler." Troy chuckled at his joke. Mia found her boyish charm cute. She walked towards the bed, deciding to go with the flow rather than over-thinking.

Troy followed suit on his side of the bed. They switched off the lights, and the room fell into semi-darkness.

Ylli and Erag heard the conversation turn into whispers and grunts.

Erag rolled his eyes.

"That tiny thing has so much power," Ylli put in with a grin.

Erag ignored the double entendre and lowered the volume. This part wasn't necessary for their job.

. . .

Twenty minutes later, the two men looked at each other as the room finally went silent.

Their guests were asleep.

CHAPTER 15

US SENATOR BRIAN REED was one of the attendees at the invitation-only NSA and Armed Forces Communications Electronics Association's Mission & Acquisition Symposium.

The speaker at the podium was a renowned NSA veteran who was talking about NSA's near-term contract solicitation schedules.

Reed's phone was face down on the table in silent mode.

The first two times it vibrated, he had been intent on the ongoing session and missed it.

The third time around, his eyes wandered to the reflection on the glass-top table, mirroring the phone light.

. . .

He partially raised the phone and peeked. It was Mia, his daughter.

He pressed the "accept call" button while getting up from his seat.

Eyes turned at the creaking of his chair and then went back to the podium. Reed walked towards the exit with his phone pressed against his ear.

CHAPTER 16

5:04 PM, **Greece (10:04 AM in the USA)**

"Dad."

"Where are you?" he asked right off the bat. It was his staple first question every time they spoke on the phone.

"Greece!"

Reed had expected her to be at college, but Mia's answer threw him off. "Greece?"

"Yes, just a short college trip."

. . .

"College trip? Why am I hearing about this only now, and why didn't Jackson tell me about it?" Jackson was Mia's college dean and also her local guardian, being Reed's childhood friend.

"He doesn't know about it."

"What! Why not?"

"I wanted to spend my birthday with my friends, away from college."

Reed paused. His anger and anxiety were replaced by guilt—he'd forgotten Mia's birthday *again*.

"Dad, it's okay. I know you're busy."

Mia had sensed the guilt in his silence. She wasn't disappointed or indifferent. Just understanding of the fact that her dad worked really hard. She knew him like the back of her hand. More than he could ever understand her. In that sense, she was like her late mother—intuitive and sensitive.

"When will you be back?" Reed asked in a softer tone. But instead of hearing Mia's response, he heard another muffled voice in the background. Then he listened to the voice mentioning Mia's name: –'Amelia Reed.'

"Mia, who is it?" Reed asked, but there was no response.

CHAPTER 17

MIA HAD BEEN STROLLING on the pavement outside the hotel's gate, wanting some time alone to speak to her father, when she heard the voice just behind her.

She turned around to see a man in a short-sleeved black t-shirt, a pair of regular blue jeans, and a pair of Air Jordans. Tattoos covered his right arm. He stepped up to her, too close for comfort.

"Who is it, Mia?" she heard her father asking on the phone.

Quickly glancing around, she found that except for the two of them, the street was deserted. The sudden fear of being alone in a foreign country gripped her senses. She had not told Troy or the others that she would be coming out of the hotel; she had meant to step out for just a few minutes. Instinctively, she tried to run, but the man grabbed her hand. Her phone fell to the ground.

"Leave me... Who are...?" She yelled and turned around to run.

Like a coiled python, the man wrapped his arm around her neck from behind, tilting her head to the right. A syringe kissed the exposed left side of her neck. She felt nothing for a second, and then the world started spinning. Her legs gave way under her, and she would have crumpled to the pavement, but the man caught her. The last thing she felt was the sensation of being carried, and then everything went black.

CHAPTER 18

YLLI LIFTED the girl in his brawny arms and walked towards the SUV that had driven up beside them. Erag quickly got out and opened the trunk. Ylli put Mia inside and covered her with a blanket.

Closing the back door, Erag looked around to see if anyone had seen them stuffing Mia's frail body in the trunk. The street was empty. There was no one to stop them or rat on them.

Ylli went back and grabbed her cell phone from the pavement. The last call with her father was disconnected when the phone fell, but now someone else was calling Mia.

CHAPTER 19

TROY WOKE at the shrill ringtone of this phone. Slitting his eyes, he stretched his hand, and his fingers touched the screen of this iPhone.

It was Dan.

"Sleeping?"

"Not anymore," Troy responded in a groggy voice.

"Check the time."

Troy checked his iPhone. It was ten past five.

. . .

"Tonight's plan is still on, right?" Dan asked.

"Yes."

"Is Mia up?"

Troy looked at her side of the bed. She wasn't there.

"I guess," he said.

"You guess?"

"She's not here."

"Then?" Dan asked.

"Then, I don't know. Hang up. I'll call you." Troy said, annoyed, and disconnected the call.

"Mia," he called. She wasn't in the room. "Mia!" he called louder. There was no response from the bathroom either.

. . .

He checked his phone. No messages. He dialed her number. After two rings, the phone was disconnected with no answer from her side. He dialed again. This time the phone was switched off.

Troy sat up. Mia had disconnected his call and then switched off her cell phone.

Had he done something wrong?

He understood that the sex had not gone as expected, but they had both been tired, and Mia hadn't made a fuss or anything about it. They had, in fact, kissed and fondled for almost twenty minutes before Troy lost steam. He knew the reason was the long journey and probably the jet lag, but it was nothing that couldn't be sorted out when they would be rested.

Had Mia gone for a walk? Or was she with Lisa or Charlotte?

Girls talk, and if Mia had discussed him with either of the girls, it would soon spill over to Dan and Lucas. That would be damning to his college reputation.

Troy got out of bed with a groan. But, whatever it was, he had to find Mia and hopefully have a private word with her to sort things out before anyone else butted in.

. . .

Deep within, he had a sinking feeling that this trip had got off to a terrible start.

CHAPTER 20

"MIA?...MIA!" Reed could hear Mia yelling in the background and a scream that was abruptly cut off. Then, a loud thump and the call disconnected.

Reed stared at the phone in his hand for a second, then redialled Mia's number. First, he got a busy tone, and then the phone was switched off.

CHAPTER 21

AS THE SUV'S door was shut tight, one of the other kids in the group appeared at the hotel's gate looking for Mia.

The SUV was a few yards away from him, and Ylli and Erag were still standing near the trunk. They watched Troy like curious onlookers and then moved to the front of the car.

The boy walked in their direction, but his focus wasn't on them. Erag took the driver's seat and put the Toyota into gear. Ylli took the passenger seat.

The SUV was about to move when Troy's hand appeared at the passenger window. They weren't expecting it, and they both were startled.

. . .

"Have you seen this girl?" The boy was showing them a photo of him and Mia.

Ylli shook his head.

"Please look closely."

"No English," Erag said with a lot of hand gestures.

"Oh..." The boy stepped away from the window, already looking further down the road.

The SUV pulled away from the curb, and as they drove away, they could see his receding figure in the rearview mirror, still searching for Mia.

CHAPTER 22

REED WAS STANDING in the lobby, still anxiously trying to reach Mia when the auditorium door opened and people started to exit. The speech was probably over.

"Brian." Hearing a familiar voice, Reed looked up to see William Helms, the director of the NSA.

Reed and Helms had been casual acquaintances during their college days when they had been on opposing basketball teams, but they had lost touch since. They knew of each other as they worked for the same government. The only difference was Helms was more or less a constant figure in the NSA, while Reed had to face the loyalty test from his voters every few years.

Helms had seen Reed in the conference and made a mental note to catch up with him before the forum ended. But as he neared him, he saw the lost look on Reed's face, and instead of saying '*How are you*?', he intuitively asked, "Is everything alright?"

Reed had no idea how to respond to this. He was still grappling with the fact that somewhere in a foreign land, something had happened to his only daughter.

Helms stopped closer to Reed and, putting his hand on his right shoulder, asked, "What happened, Brian?"

The touch was sympathetic and friendly, and this time Reed couldn't control himself. His voice choked with tears. Finally, the only word he could get out was: Mia.

CHAPTER 23

ERAG DROVE the SUV into a deserted alley not far from the hotel.

Even though the street from where they had abducted Mia was deserted, there had been CCTV cameras outside the hotel. And even though the SUV was stolen and couldn't be traced back to them, they still needed to get rid of it before it appeared on the police's radar and spelled trouble for them.

Everything was going as planned. There had not been a single glitch, and once they would get rid of the SUV, the last thing that could get them into trouble would be gone.

The SUV stopped behind a parked Mercedes Benz C Class Sedan. This was Erag's choice, who had a penchant for German wheels.

. . .

He got out of the SUV and walked to the sedan. Opening the trunk, he checked to see if there was anything that still needed his attention. The trunk space was lined with a plastic sheet just like in the SUV, so they could easily remove any traces of Mia's hair or body tissues once she was delivered to Marco's men.

All it would take was to get rid of the plastic sheet, followed by a thorough car wash. After that, perhaps he would sell the Merc and get himself a new one.

Once satisfied that everything was in order, he scanned the street for any stray eyes watching them. He found none.

He then signaled Ylli, who got out of the SUV and opened the back door of the SUV. This time he lifted Mia's body along with the blanket and walked towards the sedan. He put her carefully in the trunk, closed the lid, and then went up front and took the passenger seat as Erag started the engine.

CHAPTER 24

6:10 PM. **A private airstrip outside Athens**

A Learjet 35A stood silently on the tarmac, waiting for its passengers.

Erag and Ylli were waved past every security checkpoint till they reached the final barrier.

The guard behind the bulletproof glass studied the two men in the Mercedes, then keyed a number on his cell phone.

"They are here."

There was no response, and the call was disconnected.

. . .

The airstrip was private property, and the only way to gain admittance was a phone call from Taurus, the owner of the airstrip.

Today also, he was aware of the package in the trunk. It was his job to know what went through his territory so that he could get his slice in time and in full before anything left his shores. But he wasn't involved personally to approve every shipment. Only when the package involved a person, he made it a point to go through the motions himself.

Seventy-five percent of the total payment paid in advance had got the Ylli and Erag up to the final security gate. The remaining twenty-five percent would get them to the jet.

Taurus opened a secure chat server on his laptop and typed: "*Package is here*."

A red tick appeared on the message, indicating that someone had read it on the other side of the network.

Immediately after, Erag got a call on his cell phone. He listened, then nodded to Ylli. Ylli got out of the car and walked towards the trunk. Opening it, he drew the blanket back from Mia's face and turned her on her back. Switching on his phone camera, he then took a clear picture of her face. He sent the photo as instructed, closed the trunk, and got back in the car.

. . .

Erag was still on the phone, and he looked at Ylli before verifying that they had sent the photo.

The man at the other end checked his computer. The photo was in his inbox, and it matched the target.

Disconnecting the call, he clicked a few buttons to transfer the rest of Taurus' payment. Once done, he typed the confirmation on the chat server.

Taurus checked the response and then looked at his accountant to confirm the transfer.

Everyone waited as binary codes rebounded from one secure server to another, and finally, the payment was reflected on the screen.

The accountant nodded, turning his laptop towards his boss.

Satisfied, Taurus called the security guard to allow the sedan to enter the airstrip.

CHAPTER 25

ON THE TARMAC, two men waited patiently as the transactions between the various parties concluded.

Standing slightly away from the jet, they were waiting for their signal to proceed. The message came as soon as the final transaction was completed. The only thing remaining was to take custody of the package and pay the delivery boys.

They didn't have to wait long. A sedan appeared around the corner from the security check, rolled towards them, and stopped at a safe distance away.

Erag pressed a button in the car to open the trunk. Ylli opened his side of the door and got out. As he walked to the back of the sedan, one of the two men waiting near the jet followed him.

. . .

The girl was inside. The man snuck a quick look at the girl and nodded to his partner, still standing near the jet. He then bent to lift Mia out and put her over his shoulder. Walking past his partner, he climbed the stairs with Mia and disappeared inside the jet.

His partner now walked towards the sedan.

Inside the car, Erag and Ylli tensed. If things were to go south, they knew it would happen right about now, the time of payment. Erag rolled down his side of the glass, and the man bent and peered inside. Erag smiled at him tightly.

"You did well. I'll let Marco know." The man put his right hand inside his jacket, causing Erag and Ylli to instinctively reach for their own weapons, but the hand emerged from the jacket with an envelope.

Erag took the packet and glanced inside. Greenbacks worth one hundred thousand peeked at him.

"Anything else?" the man asked.

Erag nodded, not letting his relief show. "This is for you." He took out an iPhone from his back pocket. "It's hers."

. . .

The man took the phone, nodded, and stepped back from the car. It was a signal that their job was done, and it was time to leave.

As the sedan reversed, the man took out his cell phone and dialed. "The package is secured."

There was still one last thing to be done—deliver the package before the auction started.

He turned and looked at the pilot, who stood some distance away, taking the last few puffs from his cigarette.

"Let's fly," he ordered.

The pilot turned in his direction and raised his hand in acknowledgment. Then, crushing his cigarette under his boot, he strolled towards the jet.

Inside as the pilot readied the jet, the two men examined Mia's phone. Fingerprint-secured. One of them reached across the aisle where Mia lay unconscious in a seat, took her right-hand thumb, and pressed it on the phone. Unlocked.

He checked the call history. The last call had been to *Dad.*

CHAPTER 26

HELMS ESCORTED REED to a secluded conference room. Reed was near incoherent with anxiety, and Helms understood it had to do with his daughter, but before offering any help or taking any action, he needed to understand the situation completely.

As soon as they were inside, Helms sat Reed down and faced him. "Tell me exactly what's wrong."

Reed didn't know how Helms could be of help here, but then he had no clue about what had just happened. He still needed someone to make sense of all this, and Helms was the only one there.

Reed slowly started to describe what had happened—the short phone call from Greece, the voice in the background, his daughter's screams, then the call being abruptly disconnected.

. . .

Even as he spoke, it became more apparent to Reed that this nightmare was very real—Mia had been attacked, possibly abducted.

Helms heard him out patiently, and once he was done, he asked his next question: Who did Reed think could have done it?

Reed wasn't just a senator but was also the head of the Nevada Gaming Commission that controlled some of the most lucrative gaming regions in Las Vegas. He was the ultimate authority in approving or rejecting gaming licenses for new and existing gaming companies. The revenue every year, just from the Las Vegas Strip, was in billions, and when combined with the other gaming areas, then the numbers were mind boggling.

With a simple 'no,' Reed could have easily got himself in the crosshairs of some of the biggest gaming companies, many of which acted as fronts for mob bosses.

Helms wanted to rule out the obvious before zeroing in on possible targets. He got on the phone to get a team of analysts at the NSA ready for some quick data analysis. The first thing to do was zero in on the last tracked location of Mia's cell phone in Greece. They also had to get in touch with the friends she had traveled with.

As Helms was readying his team, Reed was repeatedly trying Mia's number. It was almost forty minutes since the call, and her phone was still switched off. He held his head in his hands in despair. He had lost his wife, and now if he lost his only child...

Helms was still talking to his team when Reed's phone rang. Reed started, then grabbed the phone.

The call was from Mia's number. With his heart in his throat, he put the phone on speaker, as Helms came to sit beside him.

For a few seconds, no one spoke as if each side was trying to gauge their opponent.

After some tense moments, Reed heard a heavily accented voice. "Hello, Senator."

"Who are you?" Reed's trembling voice echoed in the empty meeting room.

Helms' team of analysts at the NSA was already tracking the call, but he knew that the man on the other side was probably aware of this too.

"The guy who has your daughter."

. . .

There it was, then. Till now, there was still a glimmer of hope in Reed's mind that it would all turn out to be nothing. Just a prank by Mia and her friends. But the voice on the phone confirmed his worst fears. His daughter had been abducted. Reed broke down.

Helms had no option but to step in. "What do you want?" The call had to go on for the analysis.

"Who are you?" the abductor asked.

"Reed's assistant," Helms lied.

"What's your name?"

"David. What's yours?" Helms replied.

"David, you don't ask the questions here. I ask, and you answer. We understand each other?"

"Yes," Helms said after a pause.

"Good. Tell me what the senator is doing?"

. . .

"I didn't get you," Helms said.

"Describe how helpless he is."

"Why do you need to know that?"

"David, you ask anything anymore; his daughter will pay the price."

"He is worried for his daughter."

"And?"

"Crying."

The man laughed. "Tell him. This is just the start."

"I don't know you. I've done nothing to you. Why are you after my daughter?" Reed burst out, choking with tears.

Helms put his hand on his shoulder.

. . .

"In my country, there is a saying—Mali me mal nuk piqen, njeriu me njeriun piqen. A mountain never meets a mountain, but a man meets a man." The man paused. "Senator, you should not have challenged the Enterprise."

"Enterprise?" Reed was confused. "Which enterprise?"

"You made us bleed, and now your daughter will pay for it."

"I don't know about any enterprise! I didn't do anything to you. Please, please don't kill my daughter." Reed was pleading.

And the man laughed, "Oh, we won't be killing her, don't you worry. What will happen to her is far worse than death."

Reed blanched. "Pl...please, I'm begging you. Mia's done nothing to you."

"She has. She calls you dad." With that, the man disconnected the phone, switched it off, and threw it on the tarmac.

He looked at the pilot, who was now ready. It was time to go.

. . .

As the Learjet started moving, he looked at his watch. Almost seven-thirty.

The auction was about to start in a few hours.

CHAPTER 27

WHILE REED TRIED Mia's number repeatedly despite the consistent message that it was switched off, Helms stepped out of the room. He didn't want Reed to hear his discussion with Aaron, the lead analyst of the team at the NSA, about the call recordings.

"What's the call location?" he said into the phone as the door of the conference room shut behind him with a click.

"The area is in the outskirts of Athens. There is a private airstrip in that region that possibly could be the spot."

"Get me the details of any flight departed from there around the call's time."

. . .

"Yes, sir." There was a pause as Aaron passed the instructions to his team.

"What about the man?" Helms asked.

"The guy is Albanian. The accent is a dead match, and the proverb he used was Albanian too."

"He was talking about the Enterprise. Is it..." Helms said.

"It could be the Albanian cartel - The Enterprise."

"Bajrush Asani." Helms knew the name. Bajrush Asani was one of the most recognizable names in the crime world of the Balkans and the creator of the Enterprise.

"Yes, sir."

"I thought he had the policy to stay away from the US citizens."

"Yes, and that's why this is perplexing. Give me a moment, sir." Aaron muted his call to check something. "Sir, the most recent flight from the airstrip is a Learjet model headed to Tirana, Albania."

. . .

"Why would Asani abduct Reed's daughter?" Helms was asking this more to himself than Aaron.

"We need to ask Reed if he had any dealings with Asani or one of the gaming companies that act as a front to launder the Enterprise's money."

"Which one?"

"Admiral Regency. The Enterprise also launders money through other companies, but Admiral Regency is a gaming company and lies in the Senator's sphere of influence."

It was a shot in the dark, but this was also the lowest hanging fruit to start the investigation. If this didn't pan out, then it would be difficult to find the man who had abducted Mia and where he had taken her.

"Let me talk to Reed. I need everything about Enterprise and Admiral Regency. Send me a summary report as soon as you can."

"Yes, sir."

"Also, pull out the data of all TF-77 assets in Albania or anywhere close by."

. . .

Task Force-77, or TF-77, was a black ops unit jointly owned by the US Army and the NSA, which made the Vice Chief of Staff of the United States Army David Shelton, a four-star general and the second-highest-ranking officer in the Army, and the NSA director William Helms its joint custodians. It was summoned only when the US government needed to get people out of the most dangerous places on earth, and Helms suspected he would need its assets on this mission.

Helms walked inside the conference hall and saw Reed pacing back and forth, probably thinking of who else he should call for help.

"Bill, good that you are here," he said the minute Helms walked in. "I was thinking of calling Raborn. You must have good relations with him."

Walter Raborn was the Director of the CIA, and maybe the CIA was the best choice for this operation. But Helms also knew that the CIA under Raborn was different from what it was under his predecessor Turner's administration.

The thing was, if Mia was indeed in Albania, then the CIA would be reluctant to go fast and go all in.

And there was a reason for that.

. . .

With the fall of communism in 1991, Albania had sought closer ties with the US and introduced basic democratic reforms. But there was something else in the play, too. For a small country, Albania was gifted with substantial resources. While the south-western part of the country was rich in petroleum and natural gas, the north-eastern and central mountain regions had substantial reserves of metallic mineral deposits, including chromium, copper, and iron-nickel. And this was what was known; it didn't account for all the unexploited mineral wealth. It was a big pie, and the US wanted a piece of it.

One way the US was wielding its clout in Albania was through the Enterprise—the group wielded considerable political influence in Albania, which the US covertly manipulated to manage its back-channel politics.

"Brian, did you have any dealings with a company called Admiral Regency?" Helms diverted Reed's question with his own.

Hearing the name, Reed fell silent. Helms could tell that it wasn't the first time he had heard this name.

"What do you know about it?" he prodded further.

"A few months ago, this company was one of the front runners for opening a new chain of casinos."

. . .

"Was?"

"They didn't get the final approval."

"Why not?"

"I rejected it."

"Why?"

"A few months ago, I oversaw a massive crackdown on casinos involved in illegal activities in my region. During one such raid, the law enforcement agencies moved in on a small casino run by the Admiral Regency. We found damning evidence that the casino was a front for laundering drug money. Admiral Regency at the time had applied for another casino, much bigger in size and in one of the main casino belts. The company had bribed a lot of officials and bent laws to get its way. All in all, by the time the proposal reached my desk for the final decision, they had paid five hundred million dollars in bribes and such to get the license approved. They lost it all with my refusal."

"They lost five hundred million and a casino! What happened to the officials who took bribes?"

. . .

"Suspended and under various investigations."

"You know who owns this company?"

"Not really. A couple of company officials wanted to meet me before the final decision, but I shut them out. They also tried to put pressure on me through various other US senators and God-knows-who." Reed looked up at Helms. "Is that what this is all about? They did this?"

Helms nodded grimly. "Admiral Regency is one of the companies that act as a front to launder the blood money of the Enterprise - one of the biggest crime organizations in Albania. Your rejection led to the loss of five hundred million dollars of that laundered money." He paused. "Reed, the jet that took Mia from Athens is outbound to Tirana, Albania."

Reed cried. "Dear God, what have I done?" He was the reason behind her daughter's abduction.

CHAPTER 28

HELMS WAS TRYING to console Reed when his phone rang—it was Aaron.

"Brian, don't call anyone. I'll be with you in a few minutes," Helms said and stepped out of the conference room.

"Yes, Aaron."

"Asani still heads the Enterprise, but for the last couple of years, his son-in-law is managing its core business of human and drug trafficking."

"Son-in-law?"

"His name is Marcus Gjoka, aka Marco," Aaron repeated.

. . .

The name was familiar to Helms. In fact, it was the one name that had been a thorn in Helms' side for a long time. TF-77 had a thick file on Marco that was still not closed.

"There's more," Aaron continued. "We have come across intel on the darknet about a highly secret auction. Marco runs this show."

"An auction? What does he sell? Stolen artifacts?"

"No, sir," Aaron responded, his tone uncomfortable. "Young girls."

And then it hit Helms what the man had meant when he told Reed that Mia's fate would be far worse than death.

"That jet, where is it headed to in Tirana?"

“Tirana International Airport Nënë Tereza,” Aaron said.

"When will it land?"

"In less than an hour."

. . .

"What about the TF-77 assets in Albania?"

"None, but we have two in nearby countries."

"Who?"

Helms' eyes lit up at the first name. Sam Wick was one of the best TF-77 agents Helms had seen in action. A product of West-point, Wick had been handpicked for the TF-77 training program from the US Army. And from his first mission—where he had infiltrated one of the most secure prisons in the USA to break out an inmate from under the nose of the CIA, thereby becoming an instant sensation across all the US agencies—he had never failed a mission. He was the ultimate weapon against any adversary. Helms was proud that Wick was a part of the TF-77.

The next name on the list was Eddie Vicar—one of the best snipers in the world but a free-spirited guy who wasn't very fond of rules. Wick was the only one who could handle him, and they made a great team that delivered again and again. Helms assumed the reason for this was that Wick had been Eddie's first point of contact with the TF-77 unit. Wick had interviewed Eddie after he'd taken the best shot of his military career—where he'd curved the bullet's path to hit the target—and convinced him to join TF-77.

. . .

Wick had the power to convince people to do dangerous things that they otherwise wouldn't do just because Wick himself had never shied away from putting his own life on the line for a mission. And his manner made his commitment evident to even someone he was meeting for the first time.

"Send me the details of the others who went on this trip with Mia. One of them could be involved in this too."

"Yes, sir."

"And send me the file on the Enterprise and Marco. Also, find out what Marco does with the abducted girls after they land in Tirana. He can't keep the Senator's daughter for long, so how does he plan to dispose of her? We need to move quickly."

"Yes, sir."

"Thanks, Aaron," Helms said and disconnected the call. His next call was to Riley, Wick's handler.

"Riley, get Wick."

"Yes, sir."

. . .

After Riley, Helms called Marilyn, Eddie's handler.

"Sir."

"Get me Eddie."

"Yes, sir."

Helms returned to the conference room and found Reed sitting in the same defeated posture, staring at Mia's picture on his phone. The situation was beyond him, and Helms could understand that. He knew Reed would want to call Raborn for help, and he also knew that by the time the CIA would act, if they ever did, it would be too late.

He put his hand on Reed's shoulder.

"Brian, I can get Mia back." His words had significant reassuring power.

Reed looked up at him with sudden hope. "You can? What have you found? Did you talk to Raborn?"

"Brian, time is of the essence here. You and I both know that the CIA won't act fast enough to do anything here. I cannot give you more details, but I can put a plan in motion in the next thirty minutes if you give the nod."

"But..." Reed was apprehensive like any father would. This was not a movie or a novel where every time, some hero would save the day.

Helms dragged a chair beside him and sat down. His eyes were laser locked on Reed in a way that made the latter slightly uncomfortable, but that was Helms.

"Brian, we are playing a losing game here, so everything we do from here on should be focused on finding and saving Mia." Helms made a point of using the name instead of 'your daughter' to convey to Reed that he wasn't alone anymore. "The Enterprise is a target that the CIA won't touch without sitting on it for weeks, probably years, but my team can give you results in the next twenty-four hours or sooner. But if you want us to go ahead, I need you to say so unequivocally. Without your approval, nothing will move. I will try to get Mia back as soon as possible. Trust me."

His words had an integrity that made Reed hopeful. "You think you can do it?"

"Brian, I am your best bet."

. . .

Reed looked directly into Helms' eyes. He then looked back at Mia's photo on his phone. Closing his eyes, he thought for a moment. "Do it. Get my Mia back."

CHAPTER 29

Iraq

The visitor deboarded the near-empty bus two blocks away from 'Rocking Iraq.' It was a bomb shelter now turned into a club located at the far end of a strip of barren land used as a parking lot. It was the go-to place for people who wanted two things—semi-naked girls and imported booze, both a rarity in Iraq.

He was wearing a black shirt and a pair of brown jeans. Both good at hiding stains. The boots were custom-made leather.

Reaching closer to the stairs that led to the steel door entrance, ten steep steps downhill, he looked around. No one paid heed to him. Of course, this was expected at five-forty in the evening, as customers had yet to start trickling in. But there was no guard or bouncer at the door either.

. . .

He walked in without much thought. Beyond the door, the entrance was cramped, but the ceiling rose in height as he advanced further inside. The thick concrete walls made the hall soundproof. The visitor moved past the open spaces intended as a dance floor. Crossed the bar to get to the back stairwell going further down.

He had confirmed - there was an office at the rear where the back staircase ended. The door was of Sheesham wood. He turned the knob and saw three prison-hardened bouncers sprawling on a shiny couch, watching TV.

Visual of an uninvited guest made them get up.

"Who the fuck are you?" The visitor paused at the door as one of three bouncers stepped forward and stopped him before he could get inside.

"Adil Rehman. Someone told me I'd find him here."

"I asked. Who. The. Fuck. Are. You." The bouncer sounded annoyed as his hand went for his belt. The visitor noticed the outline of a handgun tucked in the man's jeans.

"Adil Rehman." The visitor repeated the name as if the man had not heard it right the first time.

. . .

"Who is it?" It was Adil who yelled from behind.

"Nobody." the bouncer responded. "I'll take care of him."

"Let him in," Adil ordered.

The visitor saw a glint of disappointment in the eyes of the bouncer. The man glared at the visitor before thoroughly patting him. This was his small win.

Adil Rehman, the club owner, sat at a large desk in the center of the room. His right-hand man - Omar - was pouring him his second shot when the visitor stepped inside. Heads turned.

The two other bouncers eyeballed the visitor. He was a stranger in Adil's office, but the reverse wasn't true. The visitor knew all five of them.

He knew that Adil was known to be many things, but primarily, he was the face of an Iran-backed Shia militia group, Kata'ib Hezbollah, believed to be responsible for more than a dozen attacks targeting US and coalition targets in Iraq in the last year alone.

"You wanted to see me, *ghabi*?" Adil asked.

. . .

Ghabi meant stupid in Arabic. The visitor didn't respond to the insult and flicked a photo onto the desk. "You know her?"

Adil glanced at the picture, and his jaw tightened almost imperceptibly.

"You want pussy, *ghabi*? It'll cost you." He looked back at the visitor. There were chuckles all around. The visitor ignored them.

"This woman. I'm here for her." He tapped the photograph on the table. "She's a reporter. A US citizen. Abducted from her home in Baghdad. I think you know where she is."

The room got quiet. The visitor had crossed several lines with just a few words.

"*Ghabi,* I think you have the wrong address." Adil was smiling but not a friendly one.

"Her family is worried. She should be home by now," The visitor stared at Adil, who studied him back.

"This whore. What's she done again?"

"Wrote an article in a newspaper."

. . .

Adil pretended to think. "Nah, doesn't ring a bell. Whoever she is, she must really know how to suck cock."

The four muscle boys laughed.

"You might need money for her. I get that." The visitor glanced around at the other guys, then pulled out some cash from his shirt pocket. "Here's a thousand US dollars if you tell me where she is."

"Thousand US dollars!" Adil quickly looked at the money, the visitor, and his men. "Can you believe this guy? Gonna give me a thousand for one pussy. Must be a Ferrari pussy..." He turned back to the visitor. "You fucking Americans. How many fucks you got left in you, man?

"Enough to pay a thousand, I guess," The visitor said.

Adil turned cancer serious. "Who the fuck you think you are? Come in here and offer money to me like I'm a pimp. A thousand. Why not a hundred thousand? Five hundred thousand? You fucking morons think you can come into my place of business and buy whatever you want! You think you set the price? Fucking reporter girl... You fucking insult me."

. . .

All eyes in the room bored into the visitor. An eternity of silence passed, then Adil burst out laughing watching his boys. "Look at him... he almost wet his pants!" His boys laughed too. Wick didn't. Adil turned to Wick. "I'm fucking with you, man. You got big balls coming here. I like that. Okay. Be Mr. White Knight. I don't give a fuck. A thousand? Those are the charges for entering my office. As for the pussy.... good luck finding it." Adil put his hand on the visitor's hand that had the cash. His eyes glinting dangerously. "Now go home and jerk off a thousand times. Then come back with another thousand grand. Forget about the girl. You are my bitch now." He let go of the visitor's hand.

The visitor turned around and walked towards the door. Adil laughed behind him. He was near the door when Omar stopped him. "Gimme your ID."

The visitor looked at him, defiance in his eyes. Adil nodded at one of the other men, who got to his feet and grabbed a six-inch blade from the table near him.

The visitor pushed past Omar and reached for the doorknob. But instead of opening it, he locked it.

The visitor's eyes moved—eyelids semi-closed. Pupils dilated like an alligator. The room suddenly shrank, and he viewed it with the detachment of a predator. The unimportant parts of the room—walls, doors, furniture, faces—faded away, leaving only what was necessary to him: the glass edge of a shelf, the tiger tattoo covering the carotid on one man's neck, the handle of a blade in another man's waistband, the outline of a gun under the third man's coat, the shot glasses at the edge of a table, ... and the fork. The bloody fork.

Weapons and targets disconnected from any sense of humanity, as his brain measured the distance between the objects and computed the time it would take him to kill everyone in the room.

All this...in the blink of ... an eye.

What happened next took the five men in the room— all armed and stronger than the visitor —entirely by surprise.

The visitor raised his elbow to push Omar away from him, snapped the glass shelf in two, grabbed the jagged edge, and hissed it through the incoming man's neck, taming the tiger. An opera of blood exploded in the air, but the visitor wasn't there to watch it. He had already moved across the room and planted the fork deep into the eye of the second man.

The others were halfway on their feet when the visitor scooped the gold shot glass from the table, ramming it into the eye socket of the third man, driving it deep enough to enter the man's brain. The man quivered like a frog in a science experiment.

. . .

Adil's hand came out of the desk drawer with a .45. The visitor moved and grabbed the gun from inside the third man's coat and pulled the trigger without taking it out, blowing Adil's hand off at the wrist. His hand, still gripping the gun, twisted to the ground like a dead bird.

The fourth man, staring at Adil's hand, didn't react in time when the visitor caught his head and jerked it until the neck snapped with a nauseating crunch.

The visitor stepped back, watching the men fall around him.

The room was now ungodly quiet.

Adil was hyperventilating on the floor. His handless arm was aspirating blood into the carpet while his good hand was fumbling with his cell phone.

The visitor crouched beside him and took Adil's phone from his hand, his eyes devoid of expression.

"Your heart is beating three times its normal rate, trying to keep your blood pressure up. That's why you're having trouble breathing. But you're losing too much blood. In thirty seconds, your heart will give up and go into cardiac arrest. Your body will shut down, and you'll slowly suffocate. So, right now, I need you to concentrate and listen to me." The visitor's voice was quiet.

. . .

Adil's wildly rolling eyes finally found the visitor.

"I want you to think about the girl. Tell me where she is, and I might save you. If you want to live, speak now."

"Yellow three-story building near Al-Kadhimiya Mosque." The words came out in gasps.

"You could have done this earlier too. Now she will live while your life will end on this filthy carpet with no one giving a shit. I also want you to understand that you died over a thousand dollars. If you had taken the money and told me where she is, everything would have been different. I gave you an out, but you didn't take it. Guys like you never do."

Adil's eyes registered the last words before they went blank.

The visitor got up and looked around. Took out his cell phone and shot a text to Riley - her handler in the TF-77 - with the address that she could relay to the US Army in Baghdad to carry out the rescue operation.

Once done, he left the room, locking the office door on his way out.

. . .

Exiting the bomb shelter, he looked around. A few cars had started to arrive. He didn't look around and walked in the opposite direction of the cars, keeping his head down.

No one stopped him. No one cared about him.

He walked for three blocks, keeping an eye out for anyone following him when his phone rang.

"Helms wants to talk," It was Riley.

"About?"

"I don't know. Will patch you in when ready."

"Okay."

Sam Wick now had to find a secluded location to take the call.

CHAPTER 30

SERBIA

Eddie was part of the team heading to the Novi Dvor - the royal residence of the President of Serbia.

He was in Serbia on the special request of the Serbian President, who had routed this request through Mark Godfrey, the US ambassador in Serbia, who was a friend of General David Shelton.

The General hadn't been very keen on using TF-77 or the US Army for this operation, but Helms had put forth the idea that this would help them plant their assets in Serbia with the backing of the Serbian President. On-ground assets always came in handy during the planning of any mission, as without them, Helms or Shelton had to pull levers they didn't want to in ordinary circumstances.

. . .

Helms had chosen Eddie for the mission. This was the kind of exposure he wanted Eddie to have to prepare him for future missions.

The task was simple. The President wanted to know how deep the tentacles of the Serbian mafia went in the government, and today would be the culmination of this mission.

Eddie was there to see the outcome of the investigation.

"Good evening, Mr. Vicar," The President greeted him in a stately manner.

"Good evening, Mr. President." Eddie felt a little out of place in the royal palace, but he didn't let his unease show. After all, he had just uncovered the rot in its very foundations.

Eddie sat back as the prosecutors read the report.

The rot unearthed traced its origins as far back as 1998. In the late summer of 1998, one of the most notorious Montenegrin criminals and a mobster from Bijelo Polje, Veselin Nikolić, was ambushed by the members of a rival gang in Belgrade when he was driving his black jeep in a three-car convoy.

. . .

Nikolić was taken to the Emergency Center of the Clinical Center of Serbia with bullets in his lung but alive. He would have survived, except for an Emergency Center doctor named Aleksandar Naumov, who was bribed by the rival gang to finish off Naumov by injecting him with a fatal cocktail. Ten days after the murder, the doctor was the owner of a new apartment.

Fast forward more than a decade, and Naumov was now the powerful Minister of Health and a close associate of the Serbian Prime Minister.

Eddie knew that the investigation would stir a political storm in Serbia with growing calls for Naumov's resignation and a trial, but Eddie would have long moved on by then.

After four hours, as he returned to his apartment, he was relieved that the months of painstaking investigation had come to an end.

He was about to open a can of beer when his handler, Marilyn's name flashed on the phone.

CHAPTER 31

HELMS LOOKED AT HIS CELL. He was expecting a call from Marilyn and Riley any minute, but first, he had to get Reed out of the room.

He looked at Reed, who was looking at him hopefully.

"Brian, there is a conference room opposite this one. You need to go and wait there."

"But I want to be here."

"Brian, you are not only a father but also a senator. Tonight, there will be dead people in a country that is our ally. Your daughter's name will come up too, so you need to maintain plausible deniability about how it happened."

. . .

"Bill, this is about Mia. I have to hear it."

"Brian, we are losing precious time with this back and forth. Get out and let me keep my promise to you." This time Helms's tone was stern.

Reed opened his mouth to argue but then sighed and nodded.

CHAPTER 32

6:27 PM

Helms walked with Reed to the conference room's door and let him out. He then waited behind the door until he heard a click that indicated that Reed had gotten inside the other room. Locking his door from inside, he rushed back to the desk. Firing up his laptop, he dialed into a secure online meeting app. Marilyn was already there, waiting for others to join.

"Patch in Riley and Aaron. I also need Wick and Eddie on this call."

"Yes, sir," Marilyn said and put herself on mute.

Helms, in the meantime, opened the summary report on the Enterprise that Aaron had sent a few minutes back. He saw

Eddie and Aaron's name flashing on the screen. They had joined the call.

"Riley is patching Wick into the call," Marilyn informed the three of them.

"Okay," Helms nodded. "Good to see you, Eddie. The Serbian President called General Shelton to thank TF-77. Good work there!"

"Thank you, sir." Eddie responded.

Two more tiles opened on the screen. Wick's name and Riley's face appeared in them. Riley was in the NSA HQ in Maryland while Wick was in a semi-dark alley.

"Everyone here? Let's get started," Helms said. "Brian Reed is a US Senator and the head of the Nevada Gaming Commission. His daughter Mia, who was on a holiday trip in Athens, was abducted around ninety minutes ago. Based on circumstantial evidence, we believe that the Enterprise, one of the biggest crime organizations in the Balkans, is behind this abduction. A few months back, they applied for casino and gaming licenses in Los Angeles for one of their subsidiary companies, Admiral Regency, that acts as a front to launder the blood money of the Enterprise. The Senator rejected the application, and his rejection possibly led to a loss of five hundred million dollars for the Enterprise. Another reason to believe Enterprise's role behind this is that the jet that took Mia from Athens is now headed for Tirana."

A photo appeared on the common video panel. Helms continued, "He is Bajrush Asani. Founder of the Enterprise. Originally, he was from Kosovo. A moderately wealthy businessman running a family-owned hotel in the Bosnian capital, Sarajevo. But behind the façade, he ran a major cocaine and heroin trafficking organization.

Asani started with the cigarette smuggling business in Kosovo during the early 1990s. During the 2001 UN Mission in Kosovo, the police confiscated contraband cigarettes belonging to him in the village of Zahać in Kosovo. The value of the cigarettes was estimated at thousands of euros. In October 2002, members of the Italian police, while trying to disrupt the main cigarette smuggling routes in Kosovo, searched Asani's business premises in Zahać and seized approximately 280 tons of cigarettes. He was taken into custody on charges of illegal tobacco production and sale of counterfeit cigarettes, but the case never went to trial. The reason was that a large part of the illicit proceeds from the cigarette sales landed in the hands of the Kosovo Liberation Army. Asani was a KLA financier, and this was one of the reasons he was able to operate in the country for so many years without getting into big trouble. When things got too hot for his liking in Kosovo, Asani moved his criminal empire to Albania. Albania had become a safe haven for Balkan criminals, and a number of powerful and well-connected individuals who had controlled the cigarette smuggling market used the same routes and connections to move into the more lucrative drug trade." Helms paused to see if anyone had any questions.

. . .

"In 2008, Asani came on the radar of the Western law enforcement agencies. In order to ensure immunity and gain political support for his criminal activities, Asani started to deliver regular packets of money to politicians in Albania to strengthen his contacts with them and with former members of the KLA. He also began to build strong ties with the Albanian police. He has since leveraged those networks to become one of the most powerful men in Albania. He is almost seventy-five now and is now looking to expand his empire beyond the Balkan region to other European countries. Currently, he is in London to meet some of Europe's biggest crime financiers over the next few days." Helms paused and pressed a button. The image changed on the screen.

"Kaplan Murat Asani, Asani's son and his natural heir. Just twenty-two, he is an art major from the Humboldt University of Berlin. Murat hates his father's business because he thinks his father neglected Murat's mother because of his business."

The image changed again.

"Agnesa Asani is Asani's daughter and is a brilliant strategist. She used to handle Asani's arms trade, but after her marriage, she is primarily focusing on being a homemaker. Her reluctance to get back in business despite having the acumen means she has relinquished her stake in the Enterprise's throne."

Helms pressed the button, and Marco's image appeared on the screen.

"Marco is Asani's son-in-law and currently handles the drug- and human-trafficking arm of the Enterprise. Under him, this segment of the business had grown exponentially. Sources tell us that he now wields as much power over the Enterprise as Asani himself. In recent times, he has gone ahead with many of his ideas without Asani's explicit consent. He was the son of Asani's driver. He has taken a lot of risks and killed a hell lot of people to reach where he is today. His rise has come at the expense of Asani's decline. He is very ambitious and desires to replace Asani in the Enterprise. Marco had also recruited his own people in key positions. With Asani out of town and Marco being in charge of the human trade business, my suspicion is that he is behind Mia's kidnapping."

"Has there been any action against the Enterprise, Asani or Marco in the past?" Eddie asked.

"No. The Enterprise as a criminal organization is important to the CIA to assert covert control over Balkan politics. But no government can afford the bad press of sacrificing its citizens, especially not the daughter of a sitting senator. This is our chance to act against Marco. Neutralizing him would effectively cripple the Enterprise."

"Do we have intel on the location where the trafficked girls are kept before they are sold or transported to the next location?"

. . .

This time Aaron answered. "According to the intel on the darknet, the Enterprise is organizing a human auction today. We believe it will be held in Tirana, where it would be easier for Marco to manage the local cops and authorities so his high-profile guests are not harassed in any way when they enter and leave the country. The girls auctioned there are probably aged between sixteen and twenty." Aaron paused.

"What do we know about these auctions, and how sure are you that the auction is today?" Wick asked.

"On probing further, we have found many high-profile names who have been traveling to Tirana since yesterday from multiple countries. An unusual occurrence as they belong from different industries and there is no high-profile event happening this week in Tirana that they could be attending. Secondly, the invitees have to deposit five million in an escrow account before appearing at the auction. My team has checked. These high-profile visitors all have money trails totaling five million each to a shell company account which is owned by the Enterprise."

"What is the probability that Marco will be at the auction?" Wick spoke for the first time.

"Less than thirty percent."

. . .

Everyone took it with a pinch of salt. It was low but not too low to abandon all hope.

"If Marco is at the auction, do we want him alive?" Wick asked.

Helms took the question. "No."

He knew getting Marco out alive would be difficult, but his larger concern was that the US government might backtrack and send him back because of some bullshit bureaucratic deal, and then it would all be a waste.

"How sure are we that Mia will be auctioned off today? The abduction could be for vengeance or blackmail." Wick said.

"We are sixty percent sure that Mia will be there," Helms replied based on the report from Aaron's team.

"What's the extraction window?" Wick asked.

"If the auction is tonight, then between 5 to 7 hours."

"How can we get in?" This time it was Eddie.

. . .

"The best way is to replace one of the invitees and send you two in their place," Aaron responded. "We have a partial list of names with photos. We have found two matches for height and weight. ." Aaron tapped a few keys on his laptop, and two images appeared on the screen. One was a young man in his mid-thirties with stubble and green eyes. The other man was in his mid-fifties—rough face, long beard, blue eyes. For Wick it was easy. Putting lenses in his eyes during a mission was irritating and could prove fatal in case the vision becomes blurry.

"Old man." Wick laid out his preference.

"Smith Jones. Five-eleven. Fifty-two years old. Divorced. US citizen. Currently in Milan, Italy. The roaster says his private jet will depart in forty-five minutes for Tirana."

"What about me?" Eddie asked.

"You will go in as his personal assistant," Aaron said.

Eddie shrugged. He didn't mind the lenses. He was more likely to need muscle than sniper vision in the auction.

"How does Jones know where to go?"

. . .

"Every client gets a code and the location of the place one hour before the auction. The code comes in a secure application that the client has to download on his phone."

"Can we mirror the phone and the application to a different phone?" Wick asked.

"The app recognizes the phone by a combination of its MAC address and the IMEI code. So even if the phone is mirrored, there is no way the application will generate or mirror the right code on the new phone. Worst case, it might trigger an alert, both the original buyer and the impersonator will be tracked, the auction will be called off and Mia will vanish for good." Aaron explained.

"It has to be Jones' phone then," Eddie said.

"Yes."

"Who do we know at the Milan airport where the jet is waiting?" Wick's question was for Helms.

"I have a few contacts that I can tap," Helms assured him.

"We need to stop Jones at the airport. Take away his cell phone. Keep him there for the next 10–12 hours. No matter what, he must not get on that jet tonight, and nor must the information get out that Jones has been detained at the airport." Wick shot his first set of asks.

"What about the jet? Marco's men could monitor its schedule," Helms pointed out.

"It will fly. We need an asset who can carry Jones' cell phone in that jet and hand it over to us in Albania. We'd also need something on which we can replicate Jones' fingerprints, a glass maybe."

"Finding an asset in Milan to smuggle out the phone will be tough, probably impossible, and the logistics will be a nightmare," Helms said, thinking aloud. He had checked and TF-77 did not have an asset there. The CIA did, but if he involved them, it would be the end of any plan. They would waste time and Marco would get away.

"What about the jet that Jones is using?" Wick asked.

"What about it?"

"It can't be a company jet," Wick said in a confident tone.

"Why not?" Aaron asked.

. . .

"If you have to smuggle a person, would you do it in your company jet?" Eddie responded this time.

Helms agreed. "Aaron, can your team find out who owns this jet and what Jones told them when he booked it. Unless the company and the pilot are also complicit, they wouldn't know that they would be smuggling a person from Albania. It would mean breaking so many laws that the owner and the pilot could spend the rest of their lives in prison."

"Okay, but how does that solve the problem of transporting the phone and Jones' fingerprints from Milan? We still need an asset to carry that phone." Aaron said.

"The carrier could be the pilot himself. Check if he has flown Jones on earlier occasions too. This might not be the first time Jones is attending this kind of an auction. We need to find something incriminating on the pilot or the company owner. If we can prove it is the go-to travel resource for such shady trips, that can be all the leverage we need.

"Got it. Do you need the company's owner involved? We can do without him, can't we?" Aaron asked.

"It would be easier if the pilot's boss were to tell him to deliver the package," Wick said.

. . .

"It will also keep the number of Italian friends we have to involve on the lower side," Helms added. He was concerned that involving Italian agencies more than necessary could lead to a leak to the other US agencies, and then the whole thing would deteriorate into a slugfest of egos.

"What about the other girls at the auction?" Wick asked.

"What do you suggest?"

"We'll need a team from the US embassy in Tirana to pick them up after the rescue. From there, they can be transferred to the embassies of their respective countries."

"Sounds good," Helms said.

"Eddie and I will tip off the local police to clean up after us when the time is right. The local police likely work in tandem with the Enterprise, so we need to make sure they act on our intel and not brush it under the carpet, or worse, alert Marco's men. So, we'll involve them only when they have nothing to salvage," Wick said.

"Ok. Riley and Marilyn will make sure that you and Eddie get passage out of your current location into Albania and then out of it. Questions?" Helms asked. There were none. "Aaron, Riley, and Marilyn, there are multiple pieces in this mission, but if we have to cover all bases, we have to work fast and in tandem. Everything needs to be ready by the time Wick lands in Albania from Iraq. He will be in the air for some two-and-a-half hours. From Serbia, Eddie would need just around an hour, so work with him wherever required. His decision will be final until Wick lands. Understood?"

"Yes, sir." Riley, Marilyn, and Aaron spoke in unison.

"Good luck," Helms said and exited the meeting. He had a lot of ground to cover, and so did everyone else.

CHAPTER 33

7:27 PM

Helms' work had just started.

His next call was to Vice Chief of Staff of the US Army, David Shelton. Helms needed the joint custodian of the TF-77 to be in the loop on this mission.

Shelton and Helms had professional relationships as far as TF-77 was concerned, but the real common ground they shared was taking care of America and its citizens' safety within and outside the country. The decision to jointly own the TF-77 hadn't been theirs, but they had agreed to take upon the additional responsibility to secure American borders in ways that were not possible either through diplomacy or via a show of strength.

. . .

From the beginning, they had followed a tacit protocol of picking up each other's call in the first instance, and if not, then returning them at the earliest. So, when Shelton, who had been about to enter a conference room, saw Helms' number flashing on his phone screen, he excused himself from the meeting for a few minutes and took the call. He knew Helms wouldn't call if it wasn't urgent.

"Director."

"General, we have a situation."

"I'm listening."

"Senator Brian Reed's daughter has been abducted in Greece and is now en route to Albania."

"What? When?" Shelton was surprised to hear the news.

"Around two hours ago."

"Who's behind it?"

"The Enterprise and probably Marcus Gjoka aka Marco."

. . .

"What's the timeline?" Shelton asked. He knew that the Enterprise was a big name in the Balkans and the opportunity to hit them was too big to miss.

"Our estimate is five to seven hours," Helms said.

"What about Raborn and the CIA?"

"You know the dynamics between Albania and the US, and the role of the CIA in that. If they get involved the girl will probably be gone forever. They will get to know this but in due time."

"Is Reed on board with this plan?"

"Yes."

"What do you have in mind?"

"I have asked Wick and Eddie from TF-77 to get to Tirana from their current locations, Iraq and Serbia."

"You'll need them airlifted."

. . .

"That will expedite things," Helms said.

"My men will be in touch with both of them and their handlers."

"General, one more thing."

"Yes?"

"We are only extracting the girl but not anyone else."

"Why?"

"The circumstances do not allow it. Besides, if we bring Marco alive to this country, he could be out in no time and back to doing whatever he is doing now."

"As long as it can't be tied to the US government or us in any way."

"You know Wick."

"That's why I'm confident it won't," Shelton said with a smile. "All the best."

. . .

"You too, General," Helms said and disconnected the phone.

CHAPTER 34

TROY, Lucas, and the others were worried. They had searched the hotel and all the nearby streets. It had been almost two hours, and there was still no sign of Mia.

Now they all were in Dan's room sitting silently.

The decision to come to Greece without informing their parents or the college now seemed like the dumbest plan ever.

"Did you guys fight?" Lisa asked Troy again.

"For the umpteenth time, no, we didn't have any fight. I was sleeping, and when I woke, she wasn't in the room. I called her. She disconnected and then turned her phone off."

. . .

"Why would she turn her phone off if there is no fight?" Charlotte demanded.

"I don't know! I can't speak for her. It's not like we've been dating for ages."

"But you shared a room," Charlotte said.

"This is ridiculous. Lucas and I could have shared a room if you weren't so eager to sleep with him." Troy was annoyed.

"What the hell?" Charlotte was red with rage.

"Easy man..." Lucas said.

The fight was getting worse with no solution on how to find Mia when Dan's phone rang. It was an unknown US number. Everyone fell silent and looked at the phone.

Who could it be?

"Hello?" Dan finally tock the call, putting it on speaker.

"Dan." It was a woman.

. . .

"Speaking." Dan looked at others who were intently listening to the conversation.

"I'm calling from Mia's father's office."

"Yes, ma'am." Dan was relieved and worried at the same time.

The phone was, in fact, from Helms' assistant Lisbon. Helms expected a feminine touch would be helpful to deal with five teens.

"We have received information that there had been a kidnapping attempt on Mia. We are working to locate her, so there is nothing to worry about. But to ensure your safety, you all should take the next flight back to home. We have also informed your parents, and you all will be receiving calls from them to manage the logistics. I will be in touch with you and your parents until you land safely in the US. Understood?"

A kidnapping? Dan did not know how to respond. It was all too much to take in. One look at his friends' faces showed him that they were equally at a loss for words. "Yes, ma'am," he said, finally.

. . .

"The next flight is in four hours. I advise you to start immediately for the airport."

"Yes, ma'am."

"I'll call you every half an hour to know your location. So do not turn off your cell."

"Yes, ma'am."

"Safe travels."

"Thanks," Dan said, and the call was disconnected. The five of them looked at each other. They were screwed on so many levels that they didn't know how to react. It was a nightmare that wasn't going to get over soon.

CHAPTER 35

AARON and his team were busy digging up dirt on the pilot, and they soon struck gold. The pilot's credit card history and bank accounts revealed some interesting details. He was making monthly transfers into two different bank accounts—one in Portugal and the other in Belarus.

Finding the addresses and the phone numbers of the owners of the two bank accounts was easy. A couple of quick calls masquerading as bank employees from the Portugal and Belarus banks made two things clear. The pilot was having an affair in Belarus, and in Portugal, he had a second wife.

And when Aaron's team combined these findings with the other information that the pilot's first wife was an Italian and still married to him, they knew that they had hit the jackpot.

They relayed this information to Helms, Wick, and Eddie.

CHAPTER 36

HELMS' next call was to Graham Rabb, the US ambassador in Rome.

Helms didn't know him very well, but he needed to build up the relationship soon to leverage it for Wick and Eddie.

"Hello?" A woman answered the call.

"This is William Helms, Director of the NSA. May I know whom I'm talking to?"

"Linda Rabb," the woman responded, and Helms quickly checked the details on Graham's family on his computer screen.

. . .

"Hello, Mrs. Rabb. We have never met, but I know your husband very well." He said, reading her profile.

"Oh... he is in the bathroom... can you leave your number, and he'll call you back?"

"I can hold if you will keep me company." Helms could have simply waited for Graham, but on instinct, he decided to do something that could potentially land him in trouble.

"Uh...sure," Linda replied.

"Mrs. Raab, I know diplomatic spouses have to wear many hats, especially in countries with language barriers."

"You are right... it's difficult, but it's great that people like you understand this."

"Well, Graham is lucky to have you by his side."

"You're flattering me, Mr. Helms," Linda laughed. "And please, it's just Linda."

"It's not flattery if it's true." Helms smiled. "Linda, actually, I called to discuss a problem, and I think you can help me with some advice."

"Sure, I would be pleased if I can help you in any way." Linda was now obligated to return the favor of that single compliment.

"There is an American businessman in Italy who, according to our intel, is involved in buying and selling teenage American girls." Helms paused as Linda gasped. "He is going to take a flight from Milan in a few minutes. Now I need your advice—should we go ahead and stop him at the airport and confront him with the evidence? But we do not have people in Italy for that, and we will need the help of diplomats like your husband to help us. Any delay will cost us heavily." Helms gave Linda some time to think.

Linda was aghast. "What kind of man buys or sells teenagers to make money? I'll talk to Graham to do whatever he can to stop this monster. You should go ahead and put him behind bars, and may God be with you. You are doing a magnificent job, saving lives."

"Who are you talking to?" Graham had just walked into the room.

Helms heard Linda say, "Your friend, William Helms. You must help him, Graham. He is trying to do a noble thing, putting a monster behind bars. Promise me you will."

"But Linda..." Graham protested.

"I don't want to hear anything... you have to help our countrymen from this monster."

"Let me talk to him." Graham walked forward and took the receiver. "Could you ask Martha to make me a cup of coffee?"

"I'm not going anywhere until you help Mr. Helms." Linda was passionate and unflinching. She put the call on the speaker. Helms could imagine Graham's face, but he didn't want to smile lest it affects his serious tone.

"Yes... Mr. Helms?" Rabb said.

"Ambassador, I need your help to stop Smith Jones from leaving Italian shores today."

"Smith Jones... the face of Jones Pharma?" Graham asked.

"Yes."

. . .

"You can't be serious, Mr. Helms!"

"I'm afraid I'm not kidding," Helms said.

"What has he done?"

"Our intel says he's involved in buying and selling American teenagers."

"That is a massive allegation on somebody like Jones. What's the proof?"

"I will share with you what we have, but right now, the important thing is to stop him before he takes his flight."

"When is the flight?"

"In thirty minutes," Helms responded quickly.

There was a pause. Then, Raab said, "Are you sure about this? If you're wrong, this can get me in soup with both the US and Italian governments ."

. . .

"It won't."

Graham weighed the consequences. The worst could be his losing his job, and the best could be a medal.

"Mr. Rabb?" Helms pressed for an answer.

Linda, too, nudged him from behind. Graham looked at his wife and then at the receiver. He was in a tough spot.

"Tell me what I'll need to do," Graham finally said after what seemed like an eternity.

CHAPTER 37

SMITH JONES—SIX FEET, fifty-two years—was a reclusive billionaire and the chairman of Jones Pharmaceuticals. Often known as the 'Vaccine King,' according to Forbes, his net worth had grown by five times in the past ten years. Although he rarely gave interviews or appeared in Media, he was known for his fancy lifestyle with mansions in New York, London, and Hong Kong, but his real hobbies lay in horses, cars, and women.

Right now, he was waiting in the VIP lounge of Milan Bergamo Airport, sipping whiskey. Tonight, he was traveling light. Accompanying him was his right hand, Rick Martel, and a fighter, Mason Gabriel.

Mason Gabriel was from a family of wrestlers and had made his professional debut at sixteen when his brother Michel had asked him to replace an injured wrestler. Already a skilled amateur wrestler, Gabriel had quickly adapted to professional wrestling, but he couldn't attain the fame he had envisioned for himself. Now he fought for wealthy people like Jones as their hired gun.

This was Jones' second time at the auction but first time attending it in person, and he knew the drill. Last time he had been suckered out of the winning bid by a Hungarian bidder. This time, with Mason at his side, he was confident he would not return empty-handed. Thinking this, he couldn't wait to get to Tirana.

He checked his cell. He had been asked to install an app for further updates. The app was ready and working, but there weren't any updates—neither the auction time nor the place. He looked at Rick - his assistant - who had just got off a call with the pilot.

"The jet will be ready in fifteen minutes," Rick said, walking up to him.

"Ask Mason to get ready," Jones said.

Rick looked at Mason. Their eyes met, and Mason understood it was almost time to leave. He got up and walked towards the restrooms.

"You think he can do it?" Rick asked the one question he had meant to ask for a long time.

. . .

"Why?"

"No reason."

"He will," Jones said. He took a large sip of whiskey and put down the glass.

By the time Mason was back, Jones was putting on his Jacket. Rick was ready with the bags. Mason grabbed his rucksack from beside the couch where he had been watching TV a while ago.

Jones walked ahead, followed by Rick and then Mason.

Their jet was in the gang hangar—used to accommodate the private planes. Departure for the gang hanger was through a separate wing.

As the trio walked towards the exit, through the double-pane glass, they could see *Ultima,* the name of their Bombardier jet, engraved in bold letters on its side.

The trio was about to go through the gate when, out of thin air, three airport officials appeared, blocking their path.

. . .

"Sir, you need to come with us," one of the officers said in a polite but stern tone.

"What the hell is this? I have a plane to catch." Jones was baffled.

"Sir, it's just standard procedure. Please cooperate." The officer was insistent. Jones looked at Rick, who seemed equally clueless. This had never happened to them, ever.

Jones looked at his Rolex and then back at the officer. "Okay, make it quick."

"This way." The officer led the way, followed by the trio. The other two officers brought up the rear.

The officer led them to an administrative zone where the walls changed from bright colors to a dull gray. The dazzling lights of the snazzy part of the airport gave way to more cost-efficient lighting. Jones could feel his spirits dampening with the decor.

The officer walked confidently ahead and paused at a metal detector.

"Please remove your wallet, phone, coins, keys, and belt. No need for shoes."

. . .

"This is ludicrous," Jones said.

"Sir, the quicker you do it, the faster we can get this over with."

"I want to talk to the person in charge here."

"Sir, he is waiting for you. If you can get this check done quickly, I'll take you to him," the officer said calmly.

Jones looked at Rick as if this was his mistake. Rick looked at the officer to avoid Jones' eyes. With no other option, Jones quickly placed his phone, wallet, keys, coins, and belt in the box. Mason and Rick did the same.

"Please walk ahead," the officer stated the obvious.

On the other side, two gloved officers stood waiting. As soon as Jones walked to the other side, one of them approached him.

"Please come with us. The lead officer is waiting for you."

"My phone and other stuff."

. . .

"Antonio will carry it into the room. Please follow me, sir." The officer was calm, but the persistence in his voice made Jones do what he was saying.

"What about them?" Jones asked, gesturing at Rick and Mason.

"They can wait outside."

"Rick, get my things, and don't fuck up this time."

"Yes... yes, sir."

Leaving the two of them, Jones followed the officer.

The officer turned into a lobby and stopped at one of the doors. Then, holding the door open, he gestured for Jones to enter.

"Please sit. I'll bring you some water," the officer said politely.

A minute later, he was back with a glass of water on a tray.

Jones took it without thinking and gulped it in one go.

. . .

The officer waited for him to finish and then extended the tray for the glass.

"My boss will be right away with you." The officer turned and left the room. As he came out, his eyes met those of the second officer who was waiting outside. The latter locked the room from the outside with a soft click.

The officer took the tray to a chamber where a man was waiting for him. He opened a transparent pouch used to bag evidence. The officer used his gloved hand to drop the glass in it. The man zipped the pouch and put it in his bag. Jones's phone was already in another pouch.

CHAPTER 38

THE BOMBARDIER LOOKED glorious in the moonlight. There was no flight attendant by the express request of his passengers. An unusual one, though. So, Giovanni, the jet's pilot, stood alone beside the plane, getting anxious.

He had expected to be in the air in the next few minutes, but his patrons still had not arrived.

Had the itinerary been changed without informing him?

His job was to fly on the whims and fancies of his customers, but he hated surprises like this.

His eyes were on the passageway that led to the gang hanger, and they lit up when he saw three shadows walking towards the exit on the other side of the glass. But before they could cross the threshold, three other men swooped in and took them away.

What had just happened?

Were they in trouble?

Was he in trouble?

The pilot was clueless and tense. All thoughts about the flight being late fled his mind.

He called his boss, the owner of the jet company. The call connected, but only briefly.

"Gio, I'm driving. I'll call you back," his boss said and disconnected the call.

Giovanni was still feeling out of place. What was going on? The guests should have been here by now.

He was still deep in thought, pacing back and forth in front of the jet, when the door leading to the airport hallway opened.

Gio stopped where he was.

. . .

A man with a leather handbag was walking towards him. He was wearing a hoodie and a pair of sunglasses even though it was evening. A surgical mask covered the rest of his face.

"You're the pilot for Mr. Smith Jones?" the man asked, nearing him.

Gio nodded.

The man took out a cell phone from his pocket and handed it to Gio.

Gio was looking at the phone in confusion when it started to ring. He looked at the man.

"It's for you," the man said impatiently.

CHAPTER 39

THE MAN WAS a local asset of the US ambassador. His prime job was to do the kind of work that Graham Rabb couldn't do himself. This was a rush job, and the briefing he'd been given had been just that—brief. He had no idea about what was being said to Gio on the call, but he saw the man's expression change from sheer incredulity to shock to fear in a matter of seconds.

When Gio returned the phone after the call had ended, his hand was shaking. "Where's the package?" he muttered.

The man took out Jones's phone from the bag. He showed it to Gio, who looked at it warily as if it was coated with anthrax.

The man wasn't interested in Gio's conscience. His job was to deliver the phone and the glass.

. . .

Once Gio seemed satisfied, the man took out a box and put the phone inside it. He then wrapped the box with paper and scotch tape. Next, he clicked photos of the box from different angles and handed the box to Gio.

"Stay," the man said. He took a few steps back and quickly took a couple of photos of Gio holding the box.

"What are you doing?" Gio wasn't ready for this.

The man ignored him and reached into his bag once more. Then, retrieving a transparent pouch with a glass in it, he handed it to a gaping Gio.

"You need to get going. When you will land, you will get a call about what to do with the package," the man said.

"What happens after this?" Gio asked the one question that mattered to him.

"Safe travels," the man said, already walking away.

Sitting in the cockpit, Gio felt a rush of fear and anxiety. His usual trips had guests, air stewardesses, champagne, and appetizers. These kinds of trips were fun, even for the pilot. But today, he was nothing more than a delivery boy running a dubious errand for someone else.

He closed his eyes and tried to calm himself. Just this one time and that's it, he comforted himself and started the engines.

The man remained at the exit gate till the jet took off. Then, as the jet's tail light dimmed in the dark, he took out his cell phone and dialed a secure line number that Raab had given him.

"Package is on its way."

Aaron, on the other end, acknowledged the message and disconnected the call.

Locked inside the room at the airport, Jones was banging on the door, cursing the airport police, and threatening to press charges.

Helms knew that Jones would do no such thing when they would tell him what they knew about his adventures with the teenage girls he smuggled from Albania using money from his accounts in the Cayman Islands and Mauritius.

CHAPTER 40

7:40 PM

It didn't take Eddie long to pack his bags. Besides a change of clothes, he packed his guns and the special custom-made boots. He had seen the boots first on Wick and was instantly drawn to them. They were pretty nifty for close-range gun battles.

As per Marilyn's message, he was to be airlifted from Camp Bondsteel. Named after the Vietnam War Medal of Honor recipient, United States Army Staff Sergeant James L. Bondsteel, it was a major base of the United States Army under KFOR command in Kosovo. Located near Ferizaj in the eastern part of Kosovo, the base served as the NATO headquarters for KFOR's Multinational Battle Group East.

The aircraft would take him to the Kuçovë Air Base in Albania, a hub of NATO forces in a region where the West and Russia had been locked in a struggle for influence for some time.

Wick, too, was scheduled to be picked up from Iraq and dropped off at the Kuçovë Air Base. It would be a three-hour journey for him, while Eddie would reach in an hour or so.

From the Kuçovë Air Base, they would have to head to Tirana, fifty-five miles by road.

CHAPTER 41

8 PM

Wick checked his watch as he strapped himself into a seat of a military aircraft at the Camp Victory Army Base, located near Baghdad International Airport. He would reach Albania in two-and-a-half hours or max three. On his way to the base, he had spoken to Eddie, who had been about to board a military aircraft in Kosovo, Serbia.

They had both received photos from Italy. The jet's name was Ultima, engraved in bold letters on its body. They also had pictures of the pilot and the package.

Wick was carrying his weapons concealed in his shoes. He knew Eddie would be wearing a similar pair. The plan was still very fluid, and everything rested on getting their hands on Jones's phone.

. . .

The mission was time-critical. In a few hours, Mia could vanish forever as so many human trafficking victims did. The success of the mission depended on everything coming together in a very short time frame.

CHAPTER 42

8:15 PM

"We have entered Albanian airspace. Twenty minutes to landing," the pilot informed the three passengers in the jet—two men and an unconscious Mia.

Hearing the announcement, the man who had carried Mia into the jet got up to check on her. She was still wrapped in the same blanket that was used by Erag and Ylli.

He didn't know her name, all they had was a photo and the fact that she was a US senator's daughter.

Lolling on the back seat, she looked calm and pretty. The man hadn't had a chance to really look at her earlier, and now he had twenty minutes.

. . .

He glanced back at his partner who was busy on his phone and then lifted the blanket from Mia. She was in a short nightdress with a V neckline and side slits. Short black-dyed hair. Small and delicate features. Tattoo of a wasp on her arm. She looked... accessible.

He extended his hand to touch her, but a voice startled him.

"What are you doing?"

"Nothing." He stepped away from Mia.

"Leave her alone and sit tight. I don't want any trouble."

The man nodded and covered Mia with the blanket again.

"She looks a lot like Lily," he said, coming back to the seat. It was a lie, but he needed something to justify what he was about to do.

"Who?"

"The girl from England."

. . .

"She is also getting auctioned tonight," he informed him.

"I didn't know that."

The pilot's voice came over the speakers. "Fasten your seat-belts. We are about to land."

CHAPTER 43

8:45 PM

When Eddie reached the Kuçovë Air Base, General David Shelton had already arranged for a jeep and an officer to take him to wherever he wanted from the base.

The drive to Tirana International Airport took forty minutes. Eddie asked the officer to wait in the airport's parking lot. He didn't want to involve him in the mission.

As the jeep turned towards the parking lot, Eddie walked towards the airport entry. His luggage was still in the jeep and being a US military vehicle, no airport security was going to flag it.

He walked into the airport using his US Army common access card and was soon anxiously biding his time in the gang hanger's waiting lounge.

CHAPTER 44

8:52 PM, **Tirana**

The two men sat silently as the jet flew through some turbulence before steadying. Mia remained strapped to her seat, wrapped in the blanket.

The men hoped she would remain unconscious until they reached the warehouse. They had been instructed to deliver her scratch-free for tonight's auction, which was still some four to five hours away.

She was going to be the night's highlight, and by the end of it, she would have a new home and a new owner.

The more experienced of the two men, who had also spoken to Reed earlier, checked his cell phone. It was almost nine. They should have reached Albania thirty minutes earlier, but the pilot had had to take a detour due to bad weather.

Still, they were on time for the auction that wouldn't start until one in the morning.

The jet touched down at one of the private airfields owned by the Enterprise. As it came to a halt, the men got up from their seats. One of them went to the back of the jet and pulled out a foldable wheelchair. He lifted it and walked towards the door, which opened with a decompressing sound.

He carried the wheelchair to the ground while his companion waited in the jet. They didn't have to wait long. A black Mitsubishi Pajero soon appeared, driving towards them with its headlights in low beam.

The man on the ground called to his companion. The other man appeared at the door carrying Mia in his arms. He descended the steps as the Pajero came to a standstill near them. He put Mia on the last seat and the other man placed the folded wheelchair beside her.

Minutes later, the Pajero exited the airstrip and accelerated down the freeway towards its destination.

CHAPTER 45

THE PHONE RANG, and Admir - Marco's right hand and the head of his security took the call.

"The package is on the way to the warehouse."

"I'll let Marco know."

Hanging up, Admir looked at Marco, who was making two neat little lines of coke on the black marble table top in front of him using the Joker from a deck of playing cards. A tightly rolled-up twenty-dollar bill sat beside the line of coke. Admir knew better than to disturb him at this moment.

Marco snorted the lines of coke and lay back on the recliner with a grunt, his eyes shut in pleasure.

After a long moment, Admir spoke, "The senator's daughter is on the way to the warehouse."

Marco opened his eyes. He stared at Admir with a dazed look, then closed his eyes again, his expression changing from relaxation to victory.

"Call the senator," he said, his eyes still closed.

Admir dialed the number from a cell phone equipped with encryption and location masking and handed it to Marco.

CHAPTER 46

THE PHONE RANG. Reed was back in the conference room with Helms. He looked at the number, then at Helms.

Helms nodded and Reed picked up the call.

"Hello," he said, trying to control his tone.

"Senator, good to hear your voice." Marco's voice was slightly wobbly.

"Who are you?"

"The man who has your daughter." Marco snorted a laugh.

. . .

Reed let out an audible sob. "What do you want?"

"Nothing."

"Nothing?"

"Once you had power over me, and you used it against me and my little project. Now I'm in your position, and I'll do whatever I can to make the rest of your life hell."

"Please, I beg you...let my daughter go. She has nothing to do with this."

"But she has, with you. And there is a price she has to pay for that."

"I made a mistake... I'm sorry... please give my girl back."

"You want your girl back?"

"Yes..."

"Talk to her owner, and he might let you have her once she's of no more use to him and his men."

. . .

"Motherf..." Reed yelled and then began to cry.

Marco grinned and handed the phone back to Admir who disconnected it.

"I'll be at the auction tonight," Marco said with a smile. "Make arrangements."

CHAPTER 47

Tirana International Airport

Seated in an inconspicuous location, Eddie re-checked the arrival list. Ultima was about to land in a few minutes. He was anxious but focused.

Before boarding the aircraft in Serbia, he had a call with Wick. The plan was largely fluid, but Eddie needed to do some ground-work. Helms and the others didn't need to know the micro stuff.

As field agents, Wick and Eddie had to improvise things from time to time based on external factors, and someone sitting far away couldn't control those factors, especially in time-sensitive missions like these.

Finally, the arrival screen showed that the Ultima had landed. Eddie got up and reached near the glass pane watching the tarmac. A smile came to his lips as he saw the jet slowly moving towards a designated parking space in the hangar, its name 'Ultima' engraved on it in bold letters.

He looked around. The VIP lounge was nearly deserted, but he intended to flush out anyone the Enterprise or Marco might have assigned to check on the incoming jet. He found no one suspicious. Maybe Marco expected his clients to be smart enough to take care of themselves, or perhaps his Albanian connections were strong enough to protect him and his guests from law enforcement agencies.

But Eddie had to be careful. He turned his attention back to the jet.

CHAPTER 48

AS THE JET'S cabin pressure decompressed, gears clicked into motion, and the door opened.

Gio stepped outside, feeling lost. In his hands were the box with the phone inside and the pouch with the glass.

With no one visible near the jet, he decided to proceed to the airport building, a short walk away.

As he neared the building, his phone rang. He hesitated, then took the call.

"Listen closely and only respond in yes or no. Understood?"

"Yes."

. . .

"At the gate, you will find a restroom to your right. Place the package in cabin seven and leave the restroom without looking back. Say yes if you understand."

"Yes." With his answer, the call was disconnected.

Gio walked in silence towards the airport gate. The restroom was actually to the right of the entrance. He looked around and found no suspicious face. There were a few people in the lounge, but no one was watching him.

He nervously walked towards the restroom.

Inside, it was deserted. He looked around and spotted cabin seven. Placing the package on the downed toilet seat, he closed the cabin door behind him and silently walked out of the restroom.

As the sound of the footsteps dimmed outside, the door of cabin twenty-one opened, and Eddie stepped out. He calmly walked across to cabin seven, picked up the box and the pouch, and placed them in his bag. He then walked back to cabin twenty-one, closed the door, and then, he waited.

Gio had not gone far from the restroom. The restroom was already deserted, so whoever had come to pick up the package would either have to enter the restroom, or if he had been hiding in one of the cabins, he would have to come out. Throughout the flight, Gio had been thinking of the photos the man in the hoodie had taken of him with the packages, photos that he feared would be used to blackmail him into running future errands. So, as insurance against this, he had decided to get a picture of his own—of the man who came to pick up the package.

He had no idea about the package he had just delivered. Whose phone was it, and what was the deal with the glass? Was it for human cloning or some nefarious hacking attempt on someone important? Sitting alone in that lounge, his mind ran in every possible direction.

Eddie had considered the possibility of Gio lingering in the airport, hoping to identify him. When he had checked the arrival time of Ultima on the gigantic TV screen, he had also noted that three jets were due to land in close succession within the next fifteen minutes. He expected the latest passengers to head for the restrooms as soon as they got through the entry gate. He sat and waited for his theory to be proven right.

CHAPTER 49

EDDIE GRASPED that the next jet had landed when he heard the first voice. Then, a second. Two men were talking to each other while washing their hands. Then, two more distinct voices could be heard. Then four more. Then, a few more. In the night's silence, their voices echoed in the restroom. Eddie opened his cabin and saw people around him. He walked towards the sink and pretended to wash his hands, his bag slung across his shoulders.

As people started to leave the washroom, Eddie walked out with the group. From the corner of his eyes, he saw Gio watching the restroom keenly. Without looking in his direction, Eddie walked away towards the main departure exit of the airport.

It took him less than ten minutes to reach the parking lot. He grabbed his luggage from the backseat of the military vehicle and thanked the officer who had driven him to the airport.

He would need another vehicle for the rest of the mission—one that could not be traced back to him or the US in any way. Wick had suggested stealing one, and the best place to find one to steal was where Eddie was standing right now—the airport's parking lot.

CHAPTER 50

INTERNATIONAL AIRPORT PARKING LOTS, anywhere in the world, are a strange place. People use them to avoid dealing with the stress of a 40-mile drive with other commuters, or having to get up extra early, or from the fear of missing their flight. So, they drive themselves and leave their cars at the airport parking lot, which, according to Eddie, was the stupidest idea.

He had seen cars getting dents, scratches, broken windows, or worse as they sat unattended for weeks, sometimes in remote parking lot locations.

But for people like him, these lots were a goldmine. Cars ready to be driven away with literally no oversight.

The parking lot was deserted of people but had hundreds of cars. Eddie turned on his flashlight and started to look for a car with a thick layer of dust.

Finally, he found an Isuzu truck that fitted the bill, plus the owner had left one of the second-row windows open. Jackpot.

Eddie crawled in through the window and hot-wired the truck. The engine purred, and he smiled. He checked the dashboard and found the parking ticket too. It was a good day.

He drove the vehicle out of the parking lot. At the exit, a man sat in a tall cabin, gawking at his mobile. Eddie slowed the truck but didn't kill the engine. He handed a bill of two hundred Albanian leks along with the receipt. The man took it, barely glancing at Eddie, scanned the ticket, and gave Eddie the change.

Eddie rolled his glass up and drove into the city of Tirana.

CHAPTER 51

SAM WICK WAS STRAPPED in his seat in the military aircraft heading towards the Kuçovë Air Base.

His Panasonic Toughbook was in his hand, now converted into a 10.1-inch tablet computer. He studied Smith Jones' image keenly and made notes of the crucial highlights on Jones' face that he needed to get just right.

Sitting alone in the cabin, Wick started to transform himself into Jones. He had no idea when and where the auction would take place, and it was prudent to save time by getting the disguise out of the way. His mastery over the art of disguise was apparent as with every stroke, his original face started to disappear, and a new man emerged.

Wick had been a top asset of the TF-77 unit for a few years now. In these years, he had executed missions and extracted targets from the most dangerous enemy strongholds. His expertise lay in simplifying intricate problems into a step-by-step plan and then executing that plan with a no-holds-barred approach.

He was in the US Army before, but disillusionment began to set in when he witnessed gross war crimes committed by his own colleagues in Afghanistan.

He began looking for an out, and when the opportunity arose, he didn't hesitate. But getting into TF-77 was almost impossible. Every year, they tested a batch of twenty applicants in a two-year recruitment process with a murderously grueling training regime. Only one of the twenty was chosen to join the TF-77, but even that wasn't a given. There had been instances when the whole batch had quit and gone back to their old jobs.

Wick's batch was special because it was the first time in the history of TF-77 that two best assets had been chosen, and Wick was the second best.

Not everyone was convinced, but by the time Wick's final test concluded, his detractors had to eat their words.

Over the years, Wick had proven that he was indeed the best in the business, and that's why his was the name that came to everyone's mind for any mission that seemed impossible. Wick always found a way to destruct the indestructible.

Marco was one such adversary. From humble beginnings almost two decades ago, Marco had risen to the top of the crime food chain, leaving a string of corpses in his wake. The Enterprise was now a formidable force and a major player in the drug and human trade. Wick knew taking out Marco would just be the beginning. The road to demolish the Enterprise would be long and arduous, but slaying the top dog would still go a long way in weakening it.

The pilot informed him that the aircraft had entered the Albanian air space. Wick put the Toughbook back in his bag-pack. He wasn't going to carry it into the battlefield. He was, in fact, going in with nothing. His thoughts shifted to the next steps of the plane after landing at the airbase. He needed a vehicle for Tirana, and an army base was the best place to borrow one from. What he didn't know was that General David Shelton had already kept one ready for him.

CHAPTER 52

EDDIE DROVE the truck towards the Kuçovë airbase. He did not intend to leave the city, but he wanted to cut Wick's distance.

He also bought a few things on the way that Wick had mentioned in his call—a can of gasoline, a barrel, and a lighter.

Once he reached somewhere near the middle of the total distance, he stopped at the side of the road. There, he took out the glass with Jones' fingerprints and carefully lifted off the fingerprints using a clear tape. Once he was satisfied with the job, he used Jones' right thumb-print on the phone's fingerprint scanner to unlock it. It worked on the third attempt.

He then opened the settings and replaced the fingerprint authentication with a numeric passcode. They couldn't be seen doing the whole fingerprint routine in front of others whenever they needed to unlock the phone. Once sure that everything was fine, he opened the application for which they had needed this phone. There was no notification as yet.

Satisfied, he turned on his parking lights. Then, cranking up the air conditioning, he checked his cell phone and dropped his location and the car's registration number, along with the information that Jones' phone had successfully been unlocked, in a message to Wick.

He then reclined his seat.

It was time to catch a quick nap.

CHAPTER 53

AS SOON AS he deboarded the aircraft, Wick found a Chevy Tahoe waiting for him. The driver saluted Wick. Wick nodded in acknowledgment and walked to the passenger side. The driver took his seat and started the engine.

"This is where I need to be." Wick showed him the coordinates he had got from Eddie.

The driver was a Private First-Class rank soldier - the backbone of the US Army. Wick's own rank was equivalent to a sergeant, although he was not actively serving in the US army.

"Yes, sir," the soldier responded, checking the coordinates.

"How long will it take?"

. . .

"Around ninety minutes, sir."

"Can you do it in less time?"

"Is that an order?"

"If you want it to be."

"I'll get us there in fifty."

"Thank you," Wick said and dialed Eddie's number. Eddie picked the call on the fifth ring.

"I'm on my way. Will see you in fifty."

"Okay," Eddie said in a groggy voice.

"Sleeping?"

"Yes."

"Okay." Wick disconnected the call and turned to the driver. "Wake me up five minutes before the destination." He, too, had decided to use the time to snooze.

It was going to be a long night.

CHAPTER 54

EDDIE HAD PARKED his truck to the side of the deserted road with the parking lights on, so any vehicle coming in his direction could spot it easily.

As promised, the soldier covered the distance in just about fifty minutes.

"Sir," he said.

Wick opened his eyes. It had been a short but effective nap. The SUV's quiet cabin and great suspension had helped. He stretched his arms and legs and looked ahead at the blinking parking lights of a car parked on the gravel on the roadside.

Wick took out his cell phone and called Eddie, who responded before the fourth ring.

. . .

Talking to him, Wick nodded. "This is me. Thanks for driving me."

"Pleasure, sir."

"One more thing, can you take this bag and keep it safe. I'll take it back from you soon?"

"Sure, sir."

Wick handed him the Toughbook, the makeup box, and his military access card.

Grabbing the rest of his stuff from the passenger seat, he opened the door on his side and got out of the SUV. Then, standing aside, he watched as the Chevy took a U-turn and disappeared down the road on its way back to the base.

Eddie was already awake and remained in the Isuzu watching as the Chevy dropped off a middle-aged man with grey hair and left.

Eddie checked the time; it was almost 11:30 PM.

. . .

"You look so different. I might have shot you," Eddie remarked as Wick settled into the front passenger seat.

"Where is it?" Wick said, not responding to Eddie's banter.

Eddie handed him Jones' unlocked phone with the application opened.

The app had two notifications that Eddie had already read. Wick opened the first message. It was the location of the auction and the time. They had an hour before it started.

The second message was the 12-digit code they needed to not get shot at the entry point.

Eddie had already keyed in the coordinates on his phone. The location was some forty miles away, but he was confident of getting there in thirty minutes because of the absence of traffic.

Wick then killed the application. He didn't want to be tracked via the application's GPS controls.

CHAPTER 55

WHEN MIA'S eyes fluttered open, the first thing she saw was a high metal ceiling. Dazed, she made a feeble attempt to get up but couldn't move. Then, with growing panic, she realized she was strapped to a chair with nylon ropes that chafed painfully on her skin as she struggled against them.

Her head was tilted backward while she was unconscious, and now she had a kink in her throat. Sorely, she moved her head and slowly observed the rest of her surroundings.

It was a large, well-lit chamber, but the place itself was more like the interiors of a shipping container, with steel walls and just one door that was shut.

At one of the corners were two stout women fussing busily over another girl who was also strapped to a chair in front of a mirror.

Mia saw her head bobbing from one side to the other. All three had their backs at her, and they were unusually quiet.

Who were these people?

Where was she?

How had she got here?

The last thing she remembered was being in Athens, at the hotel. They had landed in Athens this morning... or was it some other day? She wasn't sure of anything. How much time had passed? Was she still in Athens or somewhere else?

Her head ached as she tried to make sense of her situation. With every passing moment, she was also growing aware of her physical discomfort. She was thirsty and also needed to pee. Her body was aching, too, especially her back and neck. She looked at herself and recognized the nightdress. It was the same one she had been wearing in the hotel—when she had come out to call her dad.

And then it hit her.

The tattooed man who had tapped her from behind... the cloth he had held to her mouth... before everything went blank.

. . .

Even as the realization of her abduction sank in, Mia saw one of the two women turn towards her.

Seeing that Mia was awake, she tapped her colleague's shoulder. They looked at her and spoke between themselves in a language Mia didn't understand.

Then one of the women went to the door and knocked on it. After a few minutes, the door opened, and a man entered. The woman told him something, and the man looked at Mia. He then asked something to them, and this time the second woman responded.

The man stepped ahead and checked Mia's ropes. Satisfied, he went over to the other girl, who was still sitting quietly in front of the mirror.

After inspecting her, the man summoned someone else from outside. Another man entered the room. The two men spoke briefly between themselves and then walked over to the girl in front of the mirror. The two of them then lifted the girl along with the chair.

They put the chair down beside Mia but out of Mia's reach.

Mia looked at the girl. There was a name tag on her chest: Lily (UK).

. . .

The men then turned to Mia. And that was the moment when Mia started to scream. The men seemed unperturbed as they lifted Mia along with her chair. She struggled, but the nylon rope held her firmly in place. Finally, the men put her down in front of the mirror.

Then, to Mia's horror, one of the men took out a vial and a syringe from his inner pocket. As he readied the injection, he nodded at the other man, who grabbed Mia's left arm and held it ready for the syringe.

Mia was screaming at the top of her voice, but the men remained focused on their job at hand. As the contents of the syringe entered Mia's body, her voice turned feeble, and her body lost all its strength. As her head lolled to one side, one of the men instructed the two women to start working on her.

The auction was about to start.

CHAPTER 56

IT WAS PAST MIDNIGHT, the roads were empty, but Eddie didn't give in to the temptation to floor the accelerator. The chances of getting caught by the Tirana traffic police at this hour were low, but he didn't want to take chances.

Despite his measured driving, they made good time.

"We are almost there," he said to Wick, thirty minutes later. "You ready?"

"We need to dispose of everything in this truck before we reach there. Find a place to park."

Eddie turned into a deserted alley and stopped the vehicle. He checked his phone. The distance was now less than a mile, and the auction was about to start in less than twenty minutes.

. . .

"Call Marilyn. Tell her we're almost there. She will inform others," Wick said. "I'm calling Helms."

Eddie nodded and dialed a number on a secure line. Marilyn picked up at once.

"We are en route to the location. Inform the others. Remain on standby."

"What about the police?" Marilyn asked.

"No action as of now. We'll take a call as the situation unfolds."

"Anything else you need?"

"Not at the moment."

"One more thing. Someone called the Senator. We suspect it to be Marco."

"And?"

. . .

"Mia will be at the auction."

"Okay," Eddie said. "What about the exit plan?"

"There is an outbound military aircraft flight scheduled for eleven in the morning tomorrow."

"Okay."

Eddie and Wick expected a speedy evacuation from Albania, but they understood that they had to make do with whatever was available.

Once they were both sure that everything was good, they got out of the truck.

Eddie grabbed a can of gasoline, a barrel, and a lighter from the trunk. They had to burn the things they didn't need anymore. The car could be checked, and they had to clean it. Putting everything in the barrel, Eddie lit it up.

They waited until the fire was doused. Wick checked. They were still on time.

. . .

Getting back in the truck, Eddie drove in the range of fifty miles an hour, keeping an eye out for any sign of the designated location. After fifteen minutes of careful driving, he finally found it. Two men, waiting near the bushes off the road in a dimly lit area. He could tell from their body language that they were armed. Wick and Eddie weren't.

One man signaled for Eddie to slow down and stop. Eddie killed the ignition. The man gestured for them to get out.

"Hands where we can see them. No sudden movements."

Wick and Eddie followed the orders.

"Names?"

They gave the names. Wick was Smith Jones. Eddie was his assistant.

"Password?"

Wick called out the twelve digits from memory. One of the men tallied the code and gave a thumbs-up sign to his partner.

Everything checked out.

. . .

They gestured for Wick and Eddie to walk forward, and as they did, four men suddenly emerged from the bushes behind them and put bags over their heads.

Wick and Eddie stumbled with surprise but did nothing in retaliation.

They were thoroughly patted down for weapons and, once the men were sure that the two were unarmed, they helped them into what seemed like the back of a truck to Wick.

The truck drove for the next twenty minutes in almost every direction. It was hard to tell if it was moving in circles, but no one helped them get off or came to take off their headcovers when it eventually stopped.

Wick and Eddie were alert, their ears attuned to every incoming sound. They heard two men talking to each other in Albanian not far from the truck. Then footsteps approached, and they heard someone yelling: "Get them in the chamber."

CHAPTER 57

IT TOOK another ten to twenty minutes of stumbling over multiple staircases before they were finally ushered into a room. They heard the click of the door being shut behind them.

Wick and Eddie waited patiently. The place was silent; there was no one in it besides them. It was Wick who removed his head-cover first and then nudged Eddie to do the same.

It was a well-lit room with full-length mirror walls - clearly one-sided mirrors, so Eddie and Wick were visible to anyone on the other side, but they were clueless about what lay outside.

They were trapped, and there was nothing they could do. If their bluff had been called, they were sitting ducks waiting to get roasted. Or was this the usual procedure that every guest had to go through before being allowed entry to the auction?

. . .

They would know soon enough.

Wick and Eddie looked around. In front of them was a table with Evian bottles, glasses, and an array of face masks.

They didn't touch the water but put on the masks. The light falling on them suddenly went black, and a gong sounded. They heard something moving, and Wick extended his right hand to find that it was the glass walls that had moved up, disappearing into the roof.

Wick and Eddie stepped forward into a large hall with many people standing in groups, everyone in a mask. They all were facing a dais at one side of the hall, where an emcee stood behind a podium.

"Ladies and gentlemen, welcome to this one-of-a-kind show. We are pleased to have you here tonight. Tonight is also special as we have the inventor of this auction, Mr. Marcus Gjoka, in the house."

The emcee's voice resounded in the hall, and the enormous TV screen in the arena showed Marco sitting on a lavish couch somewhere in the building. There was measured applause from the audience, who were keenly aware that they were in Marco's territory and it was best to stay in his good books.

. . .

When the applause died, the emcee continued, "Well, we have more good news for you, lucky folks! For tonight's live auction, we have brought something amazing from the land of dreams—the USA, no less—but more on that later. For now, we have multiple other attractions making this truly a night where you will find your 'dream-come-true woman. So, let's start with the first showcase item of the night..."

The lights dimmed further, and the spotlights moved to the center of the stage, where a girl in her late teens was sitting on a couch. By the looks of it, she was heavily drugged.

The crowd cheered. The auction had begun.

Wick and Eddie studied the stage closely, but the girl wasn't Mia. They would have to patiently endure this revolting display of human debasement until they brought Mia on stage.

One by one, girls were brought on stage, displayed, bid upon, and sold. Finally, it was down to the last girl. And there was still no sign of Mia.

CHAPTER 58

MARCO WAS on the first floor, drinking the 1992 Screaming Eagle Cabernet Sauvignon from the Napa Valley.

His four bodyguards stood in silence behind him, although his right hand and security head - Admir was missing.

In front of Marco was an 85-inch TV screen showing the live feed of the auction taking place on the floor below.

He was proud of this game he had created. The auction logistics were all handled by an efficient team working round the clock behind the scenes. Everything operated on autopilot, and he rarely needed to be in the hall.

But today was different. Today he was there to watch the sale of the Senator's daughter.

The girl named Lily from Britain got sold at $125,000. Then, as she was being led off the stage, the spotlights returned to the emcee.

"And now we present to you the final and the most spectacular offering from our treasures of beauty."

Wick and Eddie tensed imperceptibly.

Get FREE background story of Lily and how she was abducted

CHAPTER 59

"RIPE FOR LOVE; she is just seventeen. Your ultimate fantasy is about to appear on the stage." The emcee was eager, his dark, muscular frame almost about to break into a jig. The last piece of the night was the very definition of flawless beauty. She was unlike anything anyone had ever seen on this stage. He could sense the audience's growing excitement as they hung on his every word. And he played on their agony of anticipation like a pro.

"A few hours ago, she could have been a prom queen. Certified pure. She is here looking for the one who can satisfy her thirst. Who will it be?" He paused dramatically, then gestured towards the darkness at the center of the stage. "Presenting to you—Mia—from the glorious land of America."

Five spotlights lit up on cue, their narrow beams converging at the center of the stage. The silence in the room exploded into cheers.

A girl was sitting on a cushioned chair, wearing only a pair of high heels and transparent undergarments covering her assets. She squinted painfully into the blinding white light. Like every other girl who had been auctioned before her, she was seriously drugged. Her head lolled to the right.

The two women who had readied her for display had done an outstanding job. Her eyebrows were perfectly trimmed, her lips the right shade of color, and fake eyelashes magnified her beautiful amber eyes. Almost fairy-like, she looked the very picture of virgin beauty.

The emcee nodded at the two skimpily dressed teenage girls standing five steps behind the chair. They stepped forward in tandem and grabbed Mia's limp arms, lifting her to display the full extent of her body. The audience erupted in loud cheers. The excitement had risen to an unparalleled pitch, but Mia was only aware of howling shadows.

The teenage attendants moved two steps forward with Mia. The spotlight moved with them.

"Raise a cheer if you would like to see more!" the emcee shouted into the mic.

The crowd roared.

. . .

"I hear you, my dear friends, I hear you."

The two attendants turned anticlockwise and paused on his signal, exposing Mia's back to the audience. "Now tell me which ass you'd like to take?"

"MIA!... MIA!... MIA!" the shadows hollered.

"If you still don't like what you see, then you are missing the Kohinoor at its prime." The emcee was inching towards the concluding leg of his sales pitch.

The two attendants circled again in the anticlockwise direction, now facing the audience. It was time for the final hurrah. The young girl to Mia's left put her hand inside Mia's transparent bra, pulling her left breast out. The crowd went wild.

The emcee looked at the cue card. The number written on it was two hundred grand. But this was a once-in-a-lifetime opportunity for him too. Girls like Mia were a rare find. The ten percent commission he would get from her trade would see him through a very luxurious year or two.

Go for the kill, he whispered to himself. "You want her. She can be yours..." He paused tantalizingly. "For only one million!"

The crowd went silent, leaving a hollow ringing in his ears. The last girl, Lily, was sold at one hundred and twenty-five grand.

Had he overestimated the demand?

He felt a tingling sensation in his hands.

Had he ruined it?

Botching this sale—any sale—meant death. Marco didn't like unsold inventories. And if he failed to sell a perfect product like Mia, the emcee knew Marco would take a blunt saw to him. Suddenly, he was sweating. He knew Marco was watching him sweat. He could imagine his displeasure snowballing with every passing second. The emcee could hear his own heart pounding in his ears.

Somebody say something, Goddammit, he prayed.

"My master will have her." Someone had thrown his hat in the ring. An ellipsoidal reflector spotlight swung to the bidder. An Arab sheik. His associate, who had announced the bid on his behalf, stood behind him with the mic.

"And... we have a connoisseur! A million is nothing for her beauty, gentlemen. Do we have another bid?"

"Interested." Someone else had entered the ring.

Another ERS threw a slender beam at the new bidder. The man wore an exquisitely tailored suit. An expensive Hublot glittered on his wrist. His subordinate was behind him, holding the mic.

"And we have two." Suddenly the emcee could breathe. He would live and live large. He could visualize the smug smile on Marco's face.

"Do we have another?" The emcee was enthused to make it a three-way fight. A few more seconds passed. No new hands in the air.

"Ten... Nine... Eight... Seven... Six..." The emcee started the countdown. "Five... Four... Three... Two..."

"I'm in." A voice interrupted the countdown. Another ERS rotated and found a masked man with gray hair in an exquisite-looking blazer paired with a set of Calvin Klein Jeans and a pair of custom leather shoes. His hands were in his pockets. He had an athletic build. His blue eyes looked straight at the emcee.

A wiry, bespectacled geek, probably in his mid-twenties, stood beside him, looking flustered. He was just over five feet and wore a plain turquoise shirt that was one size too large for him, a pair of blue khaki pants, and some sort of custom-made leather boots. His gaze was fixed on the floor like he was looking for a lost penny or something. He seemed like a man who was the happiest standing in a corner, away from the spotlight. The uneasiness of the younger man stood in stark contrast to the overconfidence of his boss.

In that gathering of rich men, they did not stand out, but their stance was unlike others.

The emcee glanced at the small screen on the podium on which the backstage folks flashed the names of the bidders even as they checked their credentials. "Mr. Jones, glad to have you here again this year," the emcee said, addressing Wick.

He was surprised to find Jones at the auction again. The previous year, he had lost both the bid and his fighter in the auction, but last year, he had not attended the auction and instead sent a proxy to represent him.

As eyes turned towards the latest bidder, the question on everyone's mind was: who would fight on Jones' behalf? The nerdy young man standing behind Jones didn't look much like a fighter.

The same question was in Marco's mind too, as he watched the scene unfold downstairs. Had this bidder forgotten the rules, or was he messing with Marco?

Wick stood impassively, ignoring the whispering around him. His eyes moved from the emcee to Mia and spent a second longer on her before shifting back to the emcee.

"Who will fight for you? The boy?" the emcee finally asked.

The money alone had little value; it was the fight that had people hooked on this unusual auction. In this arena, throwing the hat in the ring had a literal meaning to it.

"Tonight, I'll fight," Wick responded without flinching.

This was getting ridiculous. "Mr. Jones, this is not how things work. You need to have a fighter to fight on your behalf."

"The rules say that bidders must fight it out for the prize. They can do it themselves or use a proxy." Wick announced the rules that the emcee already knew.

The emcee didn't know what to say. He couldn't determine if Jones was serious or stoned.

Was he really going to fight?

. . .

The situation was a first, not to mention perplexing. He looked toward the second floor, hoping his boss would intervene.

Marco got to his feet. Jones was turning the night into a farce. He couldn't let it happen, but he first needed someone from the audience to voice what he was thinking. It would be his way out. No one could say he'd broken his own rules if his customers wanted the same thing. He didn't have to wait too long.

The audience was also getting impatient. "Is this a joke?" someone shouted.

Marco smiled and took the cue at once. "I heard you, gentlemen, and I agree with you. We need Mr. Jones to tell us why he is wasting our time. If he doesn't have a fighter, then he must leave." His voice thundered over a loudspeaker.

"I thought rules carried some weight around here. If they are just a formality, then you are right. I should leave."

One of the cameras was now on Wick, who looked straight at it. His frame appeared on the large screen in the hall. Marco felt the intensity of his glare.

How dare he? Marco gnashed his teeth, yet he covered his anger in a hearty laugh. "You have balls, Mr. Jones. I like it. I like your insanity. And I will fulfill your wish to die in that ring. On one condition." Marco watched Jones on the screen, waiting for him to flinch or betray some sign of nervousness. He got nothing.

"You will take on the other two combatants at the same time. If you survive, you get the girl, but I would love to see your limbs being ripped from your body." His voice turned murkier. "Mr. Jones, in that cage, you are going to die a very painful death, and then I'm going to keep all your money." Marco laughed.

He didn't like being upstaged, and Jones had dared to do it in his den. He'd make sure he'd die.

"Ready the cage." He yelled.

The audience gave a muted response. The idea was a dud. Jones didn't stand a chance of surviving even a punch. Now they would have to wait for a few more minutes and see this man die before the real fight began between the two actual fighters.

"Not so fast, Mr. Marco. You are not the only one with conditions." Wick was staring straight at Marco through the camera.

"What makes you think I owe you one?"

. . .

"Because I'm going to give you the pleasure of seeing your ridiculous wish coming to fruition - to see me dead at the hands of two trained fighters. You owe me one."

Marco pondered for a moment. Jones was nuts, but there was no harm in listening. "Your last wish?" he asked with a smirk.

"If I defeat them, their owners will pay for her. I keep the girl *and* my money." Wick's tone was cold.

"Is he insane?" the sheik's assistant yelled. "This is against the house rules—"

"There are no house rules tonight." Wick shut him down instantly.

The sheik was thinking too, and a smile played on his lips. He whispered in his assistant's ear.

"We agree, on the condition that when you die, your friend will be our slave forever."

"Only for six months. For the other six months, he will be mine." The second bidder was also beaming, mic in hand.

. . .

Before Eddie could say anything, Wick nodded. Eddie looked at Wick in panic. This wasn't the plan.

"Looks like the boy doesn't agree." the sheik smiled.

Wick said nothing in response.

"I... am r-ready," Eddie's unsteady voice gave away his nervousness. He hoped Wick wouldn't get his ass handed out in the ring.

Everyone else laughed, and the focus shifted to Jones. Mia, too gazed at the hazy figure of the old man.

What was happening? She had no idea.

Her throat was burning. She needed water. Everything else could go to hell.

"The cage is ready," the emcee's voice boomed in the arena.

The spotlights shifted to a large steel cage. That was where the battle would take place. The structure sported a blue chain-link fence with a single door. The closed fence would prevent any of the fighters from climbing out of the cage.

Designed to keep the combatants confined. However, three steel ladders were attached from the outside to allow anyone to climb over the top of the cage and enter the fight anytime Marco wanted. Wick expected them to be in use during the fight.

"Let's begin the fight to the death," the emcee roared.

The audience's cheers resounded through the hall. This is what they were here for.

The two fighters stepped forward from the two camps, warming up their bodies. Wick watched them closely.

"Weighing in at one hundred and ninety-five pounds and the undisputed champion of the cage matches, please welcome the man known only as DUKE," the emcee announced.

Duke had the build of a boxer. A boxer who was now a leashed dog. There were hundreds more making less than twenty grand a year for every champion fighter who became fantastically wealthy. And passion was not enough to put food on your plate. The world had seen many boxers become paid fighters over the years.

The reception roused Duke. He waved his arms above his head to stir the audience while giving the old man a fierce stare. He bounced from one leg to the other, warming up. He was ready for another win.

"Gentlemen, give a huge round of applause to welcome our second fighter! Weighing in at one hundred and fifty pounds, undefeated in one hundred and thirty-eight fights, the best fighter Japan has ever produced—Toshio Fujiwara!"

A lean, fit Asian walked into the spotlight amidst an enormous round of applause and gave a slight bow with his hands and arms at his sides. He was a kickboxer who fought for the Triad when he was won by his current owner in a poker hand. His hardened face and cold eyes took in the competition. He had to kill the old man first and then Duke. His owner had promised him his freedom once he had delivered one hundred and fifty wins. He had twelve more to go.

He entered the cage and walked towards one corner. Duke was already inside, marking his territory at the opposite corner.

Wick studied the two fighters. With Duke, it was easy to conclude that his fighting style revolved around wrestling, but Toshio hadn't given him much to go on except that he knew kickboxing. He would find out soon enough.

Two unoccupied corners equidistant from his two opponents awaited him. His chances of surviving the dual attack were in the low single digits. He felt a sinking in his stomach as if his body was pleading with him to back out. It happened to him every time before a big moment, and he still wasn't used to it.

"Mr. Jones, are you ready to die?" the emcee asked.

Wick removed his mask, handed it to Eddie, and strode towards the ring. There was no hesitation in his stride, no reluctance. The ERS moved with him, engulfing his surroundings in darkness. He could hear sniggers and jeers. The audience was here for a show, and he was going to give them one.

The cage door was open, swinging outwards. The cool breeze from the air ducts made it oscillate with a creaking sound. Wick walked up the steps and bent to enter the ring.

The door slammed shut behind him. He walked to the corner opposite the gate. All his senses were working overtime.

"Fighters ready?" the emcee's voice boomed in the arena.

Duke and Toshio nodded. Wick didn't.

A man stepped forward with a boxing ring bell. "Fight rules. Nothing is off-limits, and the fight will only end when any two fighters are dead. Questions?"

The question was rhetorical. There was nothing to ask. There was no one to referee the fight. It was a street fight in a cage.

Duke and Toshio were already in position, having marked Wick as the common enemy.

"Gentlemen, let the massacre begin!" the emcee said, and the man with the bell rang it twice.

The audience's excitement reached the peak.

Toshio moved first. From the corner of his eye, Wick saw him get into an attacking stance. But turning to face Toshio meant showing his back to Duke, and Wick wasn't ready for that so early in the fight. Duke wasn't moving. He was probably conserving his energy. Once the old man was dead, he could quickly finish his tired opponent.

It seemed like an excellent strategy to Wick, yet he didn't turn entirely towards Toshio. The distance between him and Toshio was less than three steps, but Wick realized his opponent had stepped forward with no concrete plan. It was clear he thought of Wick as an easy target and planned to finish him off quickly.

Wick stepped forward in a straight line, maintaining an equal distance from both opponents. Toshio took one more step, and Wick suddenly changed his posture and let his opponent walk into a blazing roundhouse kick that just missed his skull. Toshio ducked in time but couldn't save himself from the next kick that came crashing into his ribs. Even before he could understand what had just happened, his body hit the mat.

The crowd was stunned into silence. It had happened so fast, no one had seen the two swift kicks, but everyone heard the loud crack of Wick's leather boot on Toshio's bones. Toshio screamed in agony. His breath was knocked out of him, but he knew giving up meant death. He used all his energy to lift himself. Wick used the momentary respite to check on Duke's position; the man was still in his corner, frozen with shock.

Wick wasn't done with Toshio yet. Wrapping his arms around Toshio's head, he held him up as he thrust a knee into his ribs. The sound was unmistakable. Multiple ribs snapped. Pain exploded in Toshio's chest. His breathing became labored. His legs were Jell-O. He wobbled as Wick placed an uppercut, sending him into the cage wall.

Duke suddenly realized that they were not even fifteen seconds into the fight, and Toshio was almost dead.

Wick had him bouncing between the cage wall and his ruthless jabs like he was working out on a punching bag rather than a person.

Cross.

Roundhouse kick.

Hook.

Hook.

Jab.

Wick shot a back kick into Toshio's midsection that drove him backward, and he hit the cage fence. His body flopped with a wet, fleshy thud to the ground. Twenty-three seconds into the game, and he was dead.

Wick wasn't even panting. He straightened, staring directly at Duke, who could barely comprehend what had just happened. The old man in the ring had just killed one of the best fighters in less than thirty seconds.

In the box, Marco felt a rush of panic. He had not planned for this.

There was a hushed silence in the hall that spoke volumes. Nobody had expected Jones—an old man—to kick a trained fighter's ass in seconds.

Marco spoke into his phone, and two of his fighters ran towards the cage. Wick had expected this. Before they could enter, he had to finish Duke; he had perhaps less than ten seconds to do it.

Duke held an attack stance, but he had mentally prepared himself to fight the Asian, not this crazy oldie. He had no strategy for this opponent, and his mind was suddenly bereft of ideas. Wick saw this as his only chance; things were changing quickly, and he had to act.

"Fight, you idiot. Kill him," the sheik yelled. Duke instinctively turned towards his boss's voice, and that was a mistake. Wick lunged forward. Duke saw him coming from the corner of his eye. He turned his head while swinging his right arm in a horizontal arc aimed at his opponent. Wick crossed both hands to block the incoming punch, but instead of deflecting it, he gripped Duke's arm. He then pushed Duke's arm away from his body and immediately brought it right back with extreme force, this time trapping Duke's head between his own hands and his right arm. Before Duke could understand what had just happened, his skull had hit the wire mesh twice in quick succession.

Dazed, Duke threw a weak left punch which missed Wick by miles. Wick let go of his head, but not his right hand. He turned it by thirty degrees in the opposite direction, and a snapping sound told him that the bones had given way. He loosened his grip and let the hand fall. Duke stumbled away from Wick, clutching his injured arm with his left hand, frightened and looking for an escape. In his desperation, he made for the exit door, turning his back on Wick, who didn't miss the chance. He grabbed Duke's skull from behind with both hands and gave it a hard jerk. The skull severed from the spinal cord without resistance. Wick released Duke's lifeless body to the ground.

But this was not over yet. He heard the cage rattling and looked up.

Marco's first fighter was at the top of the ladder, ready to jump. He had not yet realized Duke was dead. His body was already in motion. Wick moved away from Duke, giving himself room to maneuver. The fighter jumped in to find Wick waiting for him. In the couple of seconds that he took to recover from the ill-planned leap, a kick in his gut took the air out of him. Before he could recover, his body was already on the ground, rolling with pain. His screams echoed in the silent arena.

Marco's other fighter stopped at the top of the ladder, realizing he no longer had a partner to back him up. Jumping into the cage meant certain defeat, even death.

Wick looked up and recognized the hesitation. He looked back at the still-breathing fighter and landed a kick in his rib cage. Another set of bones broke.

"Open the cage," Marco ordered the emcee, who signaled the man standing near the cage. Before Wick could take the third life of the night, the door swung open.

"The fight is over, and we have a clear winner," the emcee announced, his voice muted with shock. "Smith Jones."

CHAPTER 60

OUTSIDE, the sheik and the other bidder squirmed with humiliation. They had lost not only their fighters and their money but also the chance to see Jones succumb to a painful death.

Wick landed squarely on the floor from the elevated cage. He nodded at Eddie and gestured towards the stage.

Eddie walked towards the stage where Mia was still on the chair. He jumped and landed on the dais. No-one stopped him. He helped Mia to her feet carefully, as if she was a doll. She did not resist.

"Water," she whispered in his ears.

"Water." Eddie gave the emcee a no-nonsense glare. The flustered emcee handed him a bottle of packaged water from the podium. He was still having trouble believing what had just happened.

Eddie opened the bottle and held it to Mia's lips. She emptied the bottle in seconds.

"More." Her voice now had more strength.

The emcee handed him two more bottles. Mia gulped them both down.

"Thanks," Eddie said, his voice dripping with contempt.

"W... Welcome," the emcee stuttered.

Wick, too, walked over and was now helping Eddie get Mia down from the stage when suddenly the lights came on. An elevator door opened at the center of the far-right wall.

"Well done, Mr. Jones." Marco had left his bulletproof chamber to meet Jones in person, surrounded by his bodyguards in a two-by-two formation.

Wick and Eddie got off the stage and turned to face him.

. . .

"Who are you?" Marco fired the first question, walking towards them. He knew Wick and Eddie were unarmed; that was a prerequisite to attend the auction.

"Smith Jones."

"Smith Jones is fifty-five. What you just did, No one can do this at fifty-five. So, who are you?"

"Smith Jones," Wick repeated.

"Without answering my question, you can't take her," Marco said, stopping at a safe distance from the two.

While Wick was talking to Marco, Eddie quietly steered Mia away from Marco and his men.

"I don't owe you anything. I kept my side of the bargain, and you must keep yours," Wick responded, but he could see Marco's men were ready to pull out their weapons.

"You think you can come into my den and do whatever you like?" Marco said, his tone ominous. Wick's eyes were fixed on Marco, but he was also taking in his surroundings since the lights had now come on. Eddie, standing right behind him, did the same. Four bodyguards with Marco, two at the gate. Seven bodies in total.

"I thought your words had some worth." Wick indulged him. Everyone was engrossed in their conversation, but what no one saw was that Wick was slowly moving his feet apart, giving himself room. Eddie was doing the same behind him.

"I'll ask you one last time, who are you?"

"Now," Wick said in a neutral tone.

"Yes... now." Marco thought the response was intended for him, but it was just the signal for Eddie and Wick to press a tiny lever inside their custom-made leather shoes. The lever was linked to a small groove that moved in an outward direction. Inside, two custom-made plastic guns, snuck through the metal detectors, were crammed over a spring mechanism that suddenly found space to expand. The thrust threw the guns straight up in the air. The weapons were tiny and could only carry two 9mm bullets in a single magazine. Wick and Eddie each had four shots to kill seven men. One bullet to spare.

Everything seemed to happen on autopilot. Wick and Eddie were still looking at Marco. They had timed their moves to the second and did not have to look as their hands moved to catch the guns. It all happened so fast, and in such an unexpected manner that before Marco and his men could understand what was happening, their opponents were already armed.

Before they could react, Wick had already leveled his two guns and shot one round each. Two 9 mms drilled into the skulls of the two nearest bodyguards. Eddie also fired two rounds at the men guarding the main door. None of the four bullets missed their marks.

Wick and Eddie had no intention of giving the remaining three a chance to act. Eddie shifted in his place and shot at the man to Marco's right. Wick shot the one to his left. Before Marco could draw his weapon, all his men were gone.

The spectators shuddered at the bloodbath, but no one intervened. This was not their battle. The emcee had vanished from the stage.

Marco slipped his right hand into his overcoat.

"Don't," Eddie yelled, and Marco froze, his fingers inches away from his gun.

"You still want to know who I am?" Wick asked.

"You don't know what you've done." Marco's voice was threatening.

"Don't mind, but I'm taking all the girls," Wick said.

The girls, who had been brought to the stage at the end of the auction, had been watching everything. They had just seen these two odd-looking men killing six men, and yet they instinctively trusted them.

Wick nodded to Eddie. "Round up all the girls."

"Yes," Eddie said as he picked the guns from Marco's dead bodyguards, handing two to Wick and keeping two for himself. He also disarmed Marco.

Walking over to the girls, he dialed the numbers of the local press, police, and the US embassy teams.

Marco watched as the forty-seven girls he had abducted from different countries and already sold to the highest bidders were being freed in his den, and there was nothing he could do.

Wick looked at Mia. "Let's go home. Your father is waiting for you."

. . .

"He sent you?"

"Yes," Wick said.

Tears trickled down Mia's face. *Was this for real?* Her father had given her a new life on her birthday.

Wick led her towards the exit, and the other girls followed. The onlookers parted, clearing their path to the exit. Eddie stood with his gun pointed at Marco.

"What should I do with him?" he yelled to Wick.

Wick said nothing. He was already at the door with Mia and the other girls.

"Shit... shit... shit." Eddie looked at Marco and cursed.

"You are dead men walking," Marco said, gnashing his teeth.

"You should not have said that." Eddie pressed the trigger. The last bullet from his gun left a trail of smoke behind it, even as he turned away. He didn't have to check if Marco was still breathing. He knew he would never miss a shot from that close a range.

Eddie turned to the audience and smiled. "Don't leave; the police are here to take you all to your new home."

Outside, Wick spoke to the girls. "The US Embassy team will be here soon to take you all. They will take care of your travel to your hometowns." Wick said. He checked his watch. "They should be here any minute now."

Suddenly, someone hugged him from the side. It was Lily. "Thank you." she was crying.

Wick gave a forced smile. He wasn't very good with gratitude. And then, all the girls started to thank the two men. While Eddie smiled, Wick appeared awkward.

While Eddie comforted the girls, Wick was busy thinking about the next set of steps. Everything needed to be done within a matter of hours before Wick and Eddie would move on to the base.

CHAPTER 61

THE BUSES ARRIVED ESCORTED by police cars to ensure the girls' safety on their way to the US Embassy.

Once they had seen them safely off, Eddie chose a Mercedes from Marco's cars and took the driver's seat. He checked the car's vitals, and it was all good. Then, as Wick took a seat beside him, he revved the engine.

It was almost two in the night as the cavalcade drove through the empty streets. Eddie followed the buses until they reached the junction where their ways parted. Eddie took a right and soon touched the freeway.

Wick called his handler Riley to inform her they had secured the package and Marco was dead. She would relay the news to Helms.

As they wrapped up things, there was silence in the car.

"What if you had lost? I would have been their slave for life. We should discuss these things first. You know, for clarity's sake?" Eddie complained. He had worked with Wick enough to know that he wouldn't get a definite answer, yet he pressed him occasionally to get a reaction out of him.

Wick ignored him and started to remove his makeup. Eddie looked at Wick, busy cleaning his face with wet tissues, and the urge to crack another joke about his disguise died.

He revved the engine hard.

On the passenger seat, Wick was soon done with the tissues and threw them out the window. He looked younger but tired.

Behind the facade of the wrinkled profile lay a thoughtful face with battle scars that multiple plastic surgeries had softened. His black hair blew back in the breeze. Wick rubbed his bruised hands slowly, trying to soothe the pain. It was a known side-effect of his profession, but he had seen worse. He looked out the window and found a cloudless sky. It was a full-moon night. He shut his eyes and let the moonlight caress his face. His mind was calm, content. Moments like these were rare in his profession, but nights like tonight made constantly staring death in the face seem worthwhile. All he needed now was some sleep until his flight in the morning.

EPILOGUE

LONDON

The penthouse was one of the most coveted addresses in London. The walls were covered with iconic vintage pieces and artwork from contemporary artists. Bajrush Asani, the man who had rented the place for his month-long stay, was in his bathrobe sitting alone in the plush living room. His eyes were closed, and he was deep in thought about something that had bothered him for long.

Asani was the founder of the Enterprise, and he had meetings lined up with some of Europe's biggest financiers over the next few days as he looked to expand the Enterprise beyond the Balkans.

But his mind was on something else—the succession plan. Who would handle his empire after he was gone? He had been contemplating this question for a long time and had shared his concern with only one man whom he trusted with his life, Dzjelal Berisha, his trusted long-time right hand. Asani had three names, but each one of them had its set of problems.

Murat — his son and his natural heir — was just twenty-two and still living in his fantasy land. Murat was an art major from the Humboldt University of Berlin and considered himself a dreamer. Asani had little faith that Murat could handle his vast empire and keep the growth engine running. Asani's other grouse with Murat was the latter's disdain for his father's business. However, he conveniently ignored the fact that his tuition fees and comfortable lifestyle came from the same business he so openly despised.

Agnesa, his daughter, was another name in Asani's mind. She had the acumen, but Asani couldn't see her as the mob boss. It was a man's world, and it was almost impossible for a woman to command respect from men such as those Asani dealt with. Moreover, Asani feared that after he was gone, one of his people might kill Agnes and take control of everything.

Marco was his son-in-law and currently handled the drug and human trade arms of his business. Under Marco, the Enterprise had grown exponentially. By every account, Marco seemed suitable, but Asani knew the problems there too. Marco was a top-class womanizer, and even though Asani knew all about it, he had not told Agnes—his daughter and Marco's wife—any of it.

Initially, he'd reasoned that Marco was bringing in so much more money for the Enterprise that an occasional fling could be overlooked, but Marco had taken Asani's leniency as his right. As Marco had grown stronger and his hold on the business increased, Asani had come to realize that Marco wasn't in his control anymore. Marco had formed his private army, recruiting people in critical positions. Asani was now an equal partner in the Enterprise and not its undisputed king. Now, the only way to replace Marco was through a coup, but he didn't want to do it until it was absolutely necessary. Asani's main fear was that the split loyalties between Marcos's people and those loyal to the Asani family would lead to the breakup of the Enterprise.

He was deep in thought when his phone rang. It was Dzjelal Berisha.

"Marco is dead," Berisha informed him. His tone was devoid of any emotion. It wasn't that he didn't care. It was a medical condition that made him speak in a mechanical voice with minimal facial expressions. One could never really tell what Berisha was thinking while communicating.

"How?"

"Two men infiltrated the auction and shot him."

There was a long silence as Asani chewed on the news. Marco's death had solved his main problem, but there was a code, and it had to be followed. Marco's death would have to be avenged.

"I'm leaving for Tirana. Show me their dead bodies within the next twenty-four hours. I'll personally hang them in public for everyone to see," he said at last with a resolute tone.

"It will be done," Berisha replied and disconnected the call.

Wick and Eddie didn't know that their stay in Albania had just got longer.

Get WICKED SHOT and Read What Happened Next!

A Sam Wick Universe Thriller #2

GET YOUR FREEBIES

Do not Forget to download your FREE Books at

www.thechaseaustin.com

+

Get FREE background story of Lily and how she was abducted

THANK you for reading my book. I hope you would have enjoyed it. Would you be interested in telling me your views on the story?

LEAVE A REVIEW - USA
LEAVE A REVIEW - UK
LEAVE A REVIEW - AUSTRALIA
LEAVE A REVIEW - CANADA
LEAVE A REVIEW - INDIA

Book reviews are not only important to you as a readers, but they are critically important to authors like me. As a novelist, I can tell you that I depend heavily on reviews from my readers.

They not only help others to find my books, but more importantly, they help me to improve my craft so the next book I write will be even better.

Well I am here to urge you, dear reader, to leave book reviews either on Amazon, Goodreads or BookBub.

WHERE YOU CAN WRITE REVIEW ON THE AMAZON BOOK PAGE

Click the links above and they will open the respective review pages of my book in your preferred Amazon store.

Click the button "Write a customer review" (Please note that the words might vary in your country's amazon store)

On clicking the button, you will be taken to a page where you can rate the book from 1 to 5 stars (5 being the highest) and you can write a couple of line about the book.

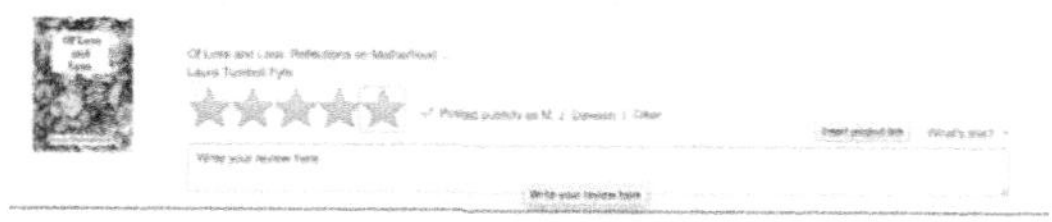

If you face any issues, please let me know at chaseaustincreative@gmail.com and I will be glad to help you with the process.

ABOUT THE AUTHOR

Thank you for reading. If you're a fan of Sam Wick, spread the word to friends, family, book clubs, and reader groups online.

I love hearing from readers. Let's connect @
www.thechaseaustin.com
chaseaustincreative@gmail.com

Join my Facebook group to get behind the scene content or follow me on Twitter, Instagram or BookBub.

To my parents who taught me to dream big.

To my wife who has been nothing but supportive every single day since we've met.

To my sister in law for helping me shape better stories.

ACKNOWLEDGEMENT

My heartfelt thanks to my **reader team** who has always been supportive of my writing and extremely helpful in rectifying mistakes that could have ruined the experience of reading this story.

Printed in Great Britain
by Amazon

47225715R00148